LOVE ON IMPACT

COSMIC KISSED

ALANA KHAN

Love on Impact in the Cosmic Kissed Series by Alana Khan
St. Petersburg, FL 33709
www.alanakhan.com
© 2021 Alana Kahn

Cover by Covers by Combs

ACKNOWLEDGMENTS

Thanks to my tribe! It takes a village to write a book.

I have my super early readers who get dailies of my writing: Dr. Lee, who I call my Developmental Editor, and my assistant Stephanie. They tell me if I'm going in the wrong direction and make sure my heroes are sexy, my heroines are loveable, and I fill the book with enough action and spice to keep my readers happy. As always thanks to my daughter, Amarra Skye, an author in her own right (write—ha ha) who never fails to help with plotting. Also huge thanks to my friend Kassie Keegan who helps with werdzing in many ways. And thanks to Kelsey Nicole Price and the Cosmic Kissed gang of writers who spent hours building this world together.

My alpha and beta teams get the book after I've completed it and they give me feedback along the way.

Also thanks to: Anuschka-Marie W., Stephanie H., Karen H ., Shardae M., Jhane, Kathy F., Christine R., Lorraine B., Kimber

J., Betty R., Anne-Marie S., Gertrude B., Kaye S., Nicole D., Sue Phillips, Holly H., Naomi B., and Corda A.

Sign up here for my free newsletter to get free chapters, deleted scenes, cover reveals and tons of free stuff and contests. Want the SEXY FREE EXTRA EPILOGUE FOR LOVE ON IMPACT? Click this link.

LOVE ON IMPACT

Abducted by space pirates to breed human women, Zoriss is one angry male when he hits atmosphere. After breaking his bonds and stealing an escape pod, he crash lands in remote Idaho. When Lumina rescues him, their bodies communicate beautifully, but with translator troubles, could he ever grow to trust her?

Lumina

It's been ninety years since the last man was born on Earth. When the government allows three alien species to help us repopulate, I set my sights on a Draalian male. It felt like winning the lottery when one literally fell from the sky. What should have been a dream turns into a nightmare when I'm stranded in a remote cave with the galaxy's most pissed off male. Because of our language barrier, I don't understand why this intriguing male is so angry, but under the covers our bodies speak eloquently.

Zoriss

Not only was I abducted and brought to another planet, my stasis capsule malfunctioned. Instead of drifting into unconsciousness, I stayed awake for three interminable months unable to move or even scratch an itch. There was a lot of time to think during my journey, but only one thought pulsed through my mind. Revenge!

Although I want to blame her, Lumina's gentle touch and affection soften my heart, and her passion sets me on fire. Learning my brother is in peril, I have to rescue him. Must I choose between my brother and the woman I've grown to love?

PROLOGUE

The year is 2180.

In 2050, an alien race visited and shared advances to our technology and the news that other races populated the galaxy.

In 2090, Earth males began dying of an unidentified, untreatable ailment dubbed AD-90, short for Adam's Destruction 2090. There hasn't been a live birth of a male on the planet for ninety years. The loss of men and the resultant social upheaval brought about many innovations such as a one-world government and changes to our social structure.

With no more viable human sperm for artificial insemination, the human race was doomed to extinction. Five years ago, the one-world government invited three alien species to Earth to save our race.

Some species are reproductively compatible, some are compatible with help. The Draalians are, to date, considered a nonbreeding companion species, although doctors across the globe are racing to rectify the problem.

Earth females must pay fees and take physical and emotional tests to apply for mates who come here voluntarily. The vetting process is rigorous for Earth females and the alien males who wish to relocate here. Both governmental and private agencies have organized to help alien males and Earth females find compatible matches, meet, and become mates.

But, like most things, nothing ever goes as planned.

1

Date: 2180
Place: Entering Earth's atmosphere

Zoriss

I thought I'd learned how to turn off my mind when I was in mandatory sniper training in the Draalian planetary army. I routinely had to bide my time for hours, once for over a day, while waiting for my target. It was hard at first, my mind tends to race, but I thought I'd mastered the ability to tolerate hours with nothing floating through my mind but my own thoughts.

Nothing prepared me for this.

I've been in stasis for, by my count, three months. Ninety days of lying here in a stasis pod without the ability to move. I can't even scratch my nose.

As a captain in the Draalian military, I've been in stasis while being transported all over the sector. You take off your clothes, climb into your pod, strap in, and a needle jabs you, putting you to sleep until the journey is complete. During that time, your nails grow, you're fed intravenously, your bodily fluids are excreted through tubing, and you awaken rested and ready for duty.

Not only was I knocked out and thrown onto this pirate vessel within hours of returning to my home planet after a five-year tour of duty, but their stasis protocol malfunctioned. Instead of putting me to sleep, I've been paralyzed but awake for this endless voyage.

My body can't move, my eyelids can't open, and I can't swallow. But it's not the physical discomfort that's been the worst part of the last ninety days, it's the mental anguish. Granted, I've forced myself to sleep longer each day, but the waking hours are still interminable.

I've played and replayed every major event of my life just to give my mind something to do. After watching those things a thousand times, I cast my mind to smaller events, trying to recall even the most mundane moments, like listening to a lecture or even walking to the refresher in the middle of the night.

After I exhausted that, I began to watch replays of the *halchuck* games I used to be addicted to. I tried to recreate every game I've ever watched, viewing them quarter by quarter, trying to remember where I was sitting when I watched them as well as who was with me and what they talked about.

By day thirty, I'd exhausted all those memories as well. For the last sixty days, I've played and replayed it all a hundred times. If I were an author, I'd have plotted a dozen books. But I'm not. The mind-numbing boredom has convinced me I've completely lost my mind.

We're evidently on our way to a planet called Earth. The assholes who abducted me have thoughtfully provided an intensive course on their customs. Not that I give a shit, but I've listened well and learned everything they taught me. I didn't need it repeated on an endless loop. I got it the first time. At least it gave my mind something to pay attention to.

There's only one thing that keeps me going. Revenge. I want to kill every fucking male on this pirate ship. This mind-torture is far worse than anything they could have inflicted upon my body. I vow with every fiber of my being that I will kill them all when they release me from stasis.

This Earth that we're bound for, I wonder what type of culture would authorize this? I've asked myself this question endlessly. If I somehow don't manage to escape, don't manage to kill my captors, if I end up on this forsaken planet, I vow I will take my wrath out on anyone who blocks my path from returning home to Draal and to my brother, my clutchmate, Zorn.

Zorn. All clutchmates are close and share a psychic link, but he and I are especially bonded, even by Draalian standards. It's like losing a limb to not feel his thoughts, his presence.

He's calmer than me, not as quick to anger. He's the strategist, I'm the one who jumps into the fray. We make a great team. If one of us had to be abducted, I'm glad it's me. Over the last three months it's given me comfort that I'm the one enduring this torture.

"Wake up, assholes," this announcement comes over the tinny speaker in my pod.

I try to open my eyes for what must be the ten millionth time since I boarded this vessel. This time my muscles respond!

Looking from side to side, I see pods on either side of me. I wonder if we've all been tortured for the last three months, or if it was just me who was the lucky one whose sleeping medication didn't work.

If they were properly drugged, the minds of the males in the pods will be slowly coming back online. Not me. My thoughts are clear. The moment after I feel the tubes retract from my body and I hear the quiet, almost imperceptible click of the pod's clear top unlatching, I'm going to break free, grab a gun from the male closest to me, and kill every motherfucking pirate on board.

I'm toward the end of a row. Looking to my left, I see an escape capsule. Although I've been planning my revenge all this time, the possibility of escape is even more appealing. I don't know how to pilot an escape capsule, but by their very nature, they have to be easy to maneuver, right?

"Wake the fuck up, you've slept long enough," assaults my ears over the speaker.

While I wait for my pod hood to open, I blissfully scratch the thousand spots I've wanted to itch for ninety days. Before the ship automatically unhooks me, I yank the hose from my primary cock, and the one that has been feeding me from my arm, ready to bolt the moment I can.

"We brought you to a planet called Earth courtesy of our little pirate operation. Earth can't produce males anymore and the women there are desperate for your cocks and your sperm. We brought you here on a little off-the-books expedition. We get paid. You get mates. They call it pussy. You get all the pussy you want." He laughs coarsely as if this wasn't a disgusting commentary on both him and the low-class females who inhabit this planet.

"While in stasis, your translator was updated with the Earth language and you've received lessons in their customs. Earth females have also wear translators. We've already held auctions. You're all bought and paid for."

Bought and paid for? What, are we now sex slaves? How do they intend to control us? The insane rage and resentment I've been harboring toward the pirates just shifted to these Earth females. They have no honor. I have no intention of ever meeting my owner. Lucky for her, because if I do, I believe she'll have a terrible, tragic accident.

The faint click of the hatch release indicates I can flee. Perfect timing. There are no guards between me and the escape capsule. I push up the clear hood of my stasis pod and leap out on feet that lost feeling months ago.

I stumble to the capsule, my muscles feeling weak as a babe's. It's hard to walk in a straight line like it always is after a long stint in stasis, but at this point, my life depends on my ability to get to that capsule.

I half walk, half lurch my way there, then pound my palm on the red button. The hiss of air accompanies the release door opening. I slide into the seat, press the red button on the dash, and the door slams shut behind me just as every guard on the vessel runs in my direction.

The whine of metal grinding on metal pierces my ears, the capsule separates from the pirate vessel, and I'm hurtling toward the green and blue ball beneath me. Earth.

If I'd just escaped a Draalian army vessel, this capsule would be programmed to home in on the safest place to touch down, then coast to a soft landing. The way this vessel is plummeting through the atmosphere, I don't think the words 'soft landing' are in my future.

Although I'm not trained in maneuvering this thing, when I try the manual controls, I realize the wires go nowhere. This capsule has been sabotaged or cannibalized for parts. Either way, I'm at the mercy of this little metal ball which is rushing to meet landfall.

My heart is thumping wildly in my chest. Even though I can finally swallow, my mouth is now too dry from fear to do so. It's an optical illusion that makes me feel the planet is rising up to meet me. I know it's just the opposite. I'm plunging, hurtling toward it at an insane rate of speed. I try to reach out to Zorn, knowing there's no way we could connect with each other over the vastness of space all the way to Draal.

"I swear by all that's holy," I bite out through gritted teeth, "if I live, I will exact vengeance."

Lumina

I normally love the steep hike down into the River of No Return Wilderness. This particular trail is so long and challenging I like to take my time. But I'm hurrying today—for good reason.

It's interesting being a vet out in the hinterlands of what used to be called Idaho. Had I followed in the footsteps of most of the other women in my veterinary class, I'd be sitting in a nicely furnished office, practicing in a large city. I've never been like most other women.

Yes, I treat dogs and cats, sometimes birds, and the occasional reptile, but I also go on house calls to treat horses and cows. All in a day's work. Today, though, I'm on my way to a rescue.

Marybeth Elkin's daughter was playing with her drone and spied a moose calf floundering in the river. When she sent me the footage via comms, it looked like the poor thing had gotten tangled in some antique barbed wire. The pictures were grainy, but it looked like it had struggled its forelegs into a tight, possibly deadly binding, then couldn't gain traction to climb up the steep sides of the canyon.

To traverse this inhospitable wilderness, I'm wearing sturdy gloves and knee-high leather gaiters over my jeans. If I hadn't been smart enough to come prepared, my palms and legs would be sliced to bits by the sharp brambles by now.

I work my way down the craggy hill on the lookout for the calf. I'm trying to get as many miles under my belt as possible before nightfall.

I shouldn't be here. I know that. It's the twenty-first of October, far too late in the year to risk traveling here, especially alone. Mine was the only car in the parking lot for good reason—wise people don't explore here for pleasure this late in the season.

Thick, heavy snows have been known to blanket this canyon as early as mid-September, and although snow that early is unusual, it's not remarkable at all for blizzards to hit this time of year.

I just couldn't watch that footage of the desperate calf struggling against its bonds and not try to save it. I could almost hear its forlorn bleats over the silent pictures as I watched them. As the area's only vet, I figured the little guy's choice was either rescue by me or death.

Finally, my hiking boots touch the gravel at the bottom of the cliff and I strike off toward the east where the animal was last seen. After the long hike down, my backpack feels like it weighs a hundred pounds. Although it was foolish to come this late in the season, I'm not dumb. I came prepared to stay awhile in case the animal needed treatment and I had to spend a few nights.

Why I'm still carrying the dead weight of my comm bracelet, though, is another question altogether. Despite the fact that every square inch of Earth has supposedly been covered by satellites for the last century or more, no signal penetrates between the rocky walls of the River of No Return's steepest canyon.

Since I have a comm unit that's no more helpful than a brick, I use the old-fashioned compass my mom taught me to use. I walk with confidence, knowing I'm heading in the right direction.

Holy shit! What is that noise? It's straight out of one of the sci-fi movies I love to watch. The fiery whoosh of something big plummeting to earth draws my attention toward the heavens. A moment later, the impact of a crash rumbles beneath my feet. The fireball leaves no question as to where the explosion occurred. Running now, I tear my backpack off and toss it to the side so I can make better time.

There's a pillar of black smoke billowing near the water ahead of me. I don't know why I'm running. This has to be an old satellite whose orbit has finally decayed, causing the thing to crash to Earth. Those relics, leftover from a previous century, have been falling to Earth so often they rarely make headlines anymore.

But for some reason, I do run. I'm driven by a sense of urgency I don't understand.

When I'm a hundred yards away, I see a silver metal ball, maybe six feet in diameter. I have no idea what those old satellites looked like, but that has to be what I'm seeing, right?

It's in shallow water which is sizzling from the intense heat of the metal ball lying in its wet embrace. I stand, paralyzed, as I debate whether I should approach or run. Has it had its final concussive explosion, or will it burst into a fireball as soon as I'm close enough to be snuffed out by the flames?

Curiosity gets the better of me and I inch closer. Although I know nothing about centuries-old satellites, I don't think that's what I'm seeing. It's round, or it used to be round before it crashed. It looks like a space-age parachute tried to slow its fall and it's completely absent the big dohickeys that were designed to send or receive signals.

With a whoosh, a round door opens. I edge closer to peer in, then slog through ankle-deep water to glimpse into the opening. All of a sudden, every awful old sci-fi movie I've ever seen flashes through my mind. Is this a spaceship? Am I safe? Are we being invaded?

Finally close enough to see into the dark confines of the tiny sphere, I take a peek. Holy shit. Is that an alien inside?

I mean, I'm not naive. I know there are aliens. We've been visited by several species starting over a hundred years ago. But they don't usually arrive in one-person fireballs from outer space.

I approach like the frightened doe I made friends with once. In fact, she was the driving reason I wanted to become a vet. As a preteen, I was reading a book out in the woods. I waited hours for her to come to me, one step at a time, always careful to keep my gaze from becoming too personal. Her velvet nose nudging my hand was a seminal moment in my life.

I sneak close enough to peer in and gasp when it's clear I'm not only seeing an alien—it's a Draalian. A naked one.

Is this an early Christmas present? Everyone in town knows I've been saving up for a Draalian mate. Hell, every time I go to the grocery store, the women at the check-out ask how my Draalian savings account is coming.

There are so few males on our planet. Not only do we have to find compatible species and do ad campaigns to encourage them to come, but the government or private agencies have to test them for mental and physical health.

The agencies then house and feed them and perform all the matchmaking tests as well. Because of the law of supply and demand, it's expensive to apply to the mating services.

Every spare penny I get goes into that fund. The extra money I make by putting calligraphic addresses on birthday and Christmas cards goes there. When I'm not busy enough at my practice, I call clients to see if I can groom their dogs for extra credits.

My mom jokes I 'drool over Draalians', and she's right.

"Stop drooling, Lumina, and get to work," I scold myself.

I reach inside the capsule in trepidation. Who knows, this guy might be playing possum and reach out and grab me. Once I get a good look at him, though, it's obvious he's not conscious. I'm not even certain he's alive.

Two fingers on his carotid answer that question. He has a pulse, but it's thready. He's going to need medical attention. I tamp down my fear and excitement and switch into professional mode. This guy doesn't have a lot of time to wait around for treatment.

There's a cave about half-a-mile back near where I dropped my backpack. I made a mental note that it would work as shelter in case I had to stay here overnight to tend the calf.

Although I can't read Draalian, I see pictograms that even an idiot could interpret on how to detach the round capsule door from the rest of the sphere. I manage to release the lock, then rock it back and forth to remove it. It bent upon impact and didn't exactly slip off as intended.

Now that the disk is curved side down in the shallows at the water's edge, I release the harness that has the male secured to the seat. After struggling to pull the Draalian out and lay him on it, I tuck his knees to his chest so the over-six-foot alien will be able to ride on the five-foot round door.

There's blood, lots of it—and it's blue. I don't want to take the time to inspect him. I've watched enough vids to be plenty worried about the craft exploding. I want to leave now, but I take an extra minute to poke around in the cabin, looking for anything that might prove helpful.

There's a box that might be a first aid kit. I grab it and toss it gently on the door. There are two thick blue blankets under the seat. I definitely want those. Draals are reptilian. They're cold-blooded and can't self-regulate their body temperature.

If I'm not mistaken, the little packages I find in a cubby are freeze-dried food. They're covered with pictures of little insects. Gross.

"Okay, big guy, let's bounce."

The door handle has a thick webbed pull attached. It's a couple of yards long, so I'll be able to more easily lug my cargo toward the cave. I'd better hustle, the sun drops like a rock out here.

Once it passes over the slim opening of the deep chasm, the light fades fast. So does the heat.

I feel the chill in the air already, so once I'm far enough from the crash site that I'm out of the explosion zone, I stop for a moment to cover him with the blankets. I take one teeny tiny moment to inspect him. I tell myself it's to see if I need to do a field dressing on him, but I was never good at lying to myself.

I'm looking at his wounds, yeah, that's what medical professionals do, but I'm also looking at *him*.

Five years ago, long after it was clear humans weren't going to birth any more male babies, the women of Earth decided to allow other species to emigrate here. We agreed upon three species to start with. The Saveet, the Zresta, and the Draal.

For some reason, it was the Draal and only the Draal that turned me on. Literally. I have a scrolling Draalian screensaver, keep daily track of the number of immigrants from that planet, and finally gave in to temptation and used some of my savings to buy a Draalian sexbot. My mouth is dry just looking at the male in front of me, and I haven't even allowed my gaze to dip below his waist.

His face is perfectly symmetrical, carrying the hallmarks of his race: flat nose, thin lips, little fangs that protrude from the upper jaw, and high cheekbones. Just as I suspected, his lack of hair makes his features even more handsome.

I tell myself I need to inspect all of him for injuries. Since he's curled on his side, I have to move his top leg to get a better look at him. My eyes spend an inordinate amount of time inspecting his genitals—the two blue cocks these males are famous for. When flaccid it's hard to see past the secondary cock resting on the primary cock which is hidden in shadows. The sight before my eyes is enough to fuel my fantasies for the rest of my lifetime.

"Lumina, you're a pervert," I scold myself even as I allow myself to drink in the sight of him for one more second.

I flip him onto his other side and see the gash. The profusely bleeding gash. Right near his cocks and dangerously close to his femoral artery. If the crash had severed his femoral artery he'd already be dead, so it's not that serious, but it's clearly been nicked.

I pull off my t-shirt and use my teeth to make enough of a hole in it to tear a three-inch wide strip along the bottom. I have a knife somewhere in my backpack, but I dropped it on the run to the crash and don't want to waste time backtracking. It's dark out now, the landscape only lit by the gleam of the three-quarter moon.

After pulling my shirt back on and kneeling at his hip, I hesitate a moment as I wonder how to attack the problem. There's no way around it, I'm going to have to touch his cocks. Swallowing hard, I slip my hand between his legs, brush both penises out of the way, and tie a quick tourniquet. I'll do a more thorough job after I get him to the cave. After tucking both blankets around him, I grab the webbed pull and trudge forward.

Because the river is shallow this time of year, I can't float him toward the cave. Mostly I pull him forward, but when my arms and shoulders ache from that position, I turn around and walk backward just to give my screaming muscles a rest.

There's enough moonlight for me to see a moose calf across the river at the water's edge. He dips his ungainly head as he takes a drink. By the dark patches on his legs which I can only assume are blood, I know with certainty this is the one I came here to save.

I'm relieved to see he escaped the restraining barbed wire on his own and his injuries don't appear serious. He takes one look at me and lopes away. I guess all the medical supplies in my back-pack can be put to a different purpose. My gaze flicks to the comatose male on the metal disc.

Walking backward, I inspect the Draalian. Such a pretty male. I don't know why I find this species so handsome, but I do. There's something about their blue scales that calls to me. This one has an interesting pattern of light and dark blue. I wonder what color his eyes are, then I imagine those eyes looking at me like he can't wait to remove my clothes and have his way with me.

The thin lips his race is known for grace his face. I've always wondered about their forked tongues, not sure if it would be sexy or have a high 'ick factor'. That remains to be seen.

He has broad shoulders sculpted by powerful, ropey muscles. There's an armband around his right bicep. The silver metal is filigreed and has a round ruby in the middle of the design. It's the only thing he's wearing.

Turning forward, it's as if all of my awareness is focused on three fingers of my right hand. The three fingers that brushed his penises when I moved them to apply the tourniquet. I know it's not right to be so focused on those two gorgeous cocks. As a doctor, I shouldn't be intrigued by a patient's genitals. Even though I'm just a vet, I should still be more professional.

I finally see the cave up ahead, my hastily tossed backpack waiting a few steps from the opening. I pull him inside, grab the small flashlight from my pack, and look for predators who might be lurking there, especially bears. I don't see anything.

I pick a spot near the rear of the cave to open the small sleeping bag I brought with me, then ease him onto it as gently as I can lug a two-hundred-pound male. Once he's settled, I drag the door outside to collect firewood.

"I'll be back," I call to my comatose Draal.

While I'm gathering firewood and tossing it on the door, I can't help but wonder why the male is here. Alien mates choose to come to Earth at our request. They come on ships and wind up in tidy barracks where they learn our customs and choose women to date. Although this isn't the way it's done, I'm closer to a Draalian than I ever thought I'd be. He's so handsome. And he's hurt. I need to hurry back and tend to him.

I return with kindling and at least a day's worth of firewood, then use the lighter from my pack to make a roaring fire.

With that source of heat and light, I pull the blankets off him and perform a complete inspection. Scales, of course, are thicker than skin, so he's not as banged up as I thought he'd be. He has cuts and scrapes all over, especially his chest.

There's a slash of blue blood on his temple, which must be why he hasn't regained consciousness. I wonder if he has brain damage, but don't have the equipment to run any tests. I'll look at that later since the leg wound is more urgent.

I open his legs wide to get good access to the deep gash near his groin, then peel off the blood-soaked t-shirt fabric I used when I field-dressed him. It's caked to his scales, but with a slight bit of pressure, I lift it off him.

Grabbing a collapsible pot from my backpack, I hurry to the rushing river outside the cave and return with enough water to clean the wound. It's deep enough to worry me. It's a wonder his artery wasn't sliced.

Draalian anatomy is probably different from ours. Well, duh, the two cocks are a dead giveaway. I'll just have to keep a close eye on this.

After another trip for clean water, I finish irrigating the wound as thoroughly as possible. Grabbing the disinfectant spray, I give him a generous dusting, then rummage in my pack for the self-adhering gauze. I consider using medi-seal to close the wound, but fear I may have to go back in to clean and disinfect again. I decide to bandage it and reassess in the morning.

If we weren't a three-hour hike down a canyon, I'd take him to a hospital where he'd be properly treated. I certainly can't carry him out, nor can I use my comm because it gets no signal.

I bend his knee so his sole is flat on the floor, which allows me to more easily wrap his upper thigh. As I do this, I wonder if he can tolerate the antibiotic I brought for the moose calf. Although I know nothing about Draalian physiology, I assume he can tolerate our medicines.

The scientists who picked the first three species to join us on Earth were looking for genetic matches so we could procreate. I heard this vast experiment referred to as Project Ark when it was in its infancy.

The other two species have produced some adorable human hybrid babies, but the jury is still out on Draalians. They haven't been able to procreate with humans yet, but there is hope for that. I'll just have to assume we have a lot of genetic similarities or they wouldn't have been among the first to emigrate to our planet.

It's an interesting irony that my planet isn't producing males anymore and Draal's population is now ninety percent male because of their global warming.

What was this guy doing here, anyway? This male was obviously traveling alone. Could he possibly have come all the way from Draal on his own in his efforts to find a female? Was he so desperate for a mate he risked life and limb in that tiny capsule? He must really want an Earth woman. How romantic.

My nostrils flare and my head tips back as I wonder about that. We have a rigorous screening process before we allow males to board transport vessels to come here. We don't want unstable, sick, or criminal mates. Could that be what this male is? Some reject who couldn't pass inspection? One who was so desperate for a mate he traveled across the galaxy on his own to find one?

"I wonder who you are," I whisper into the cave as my fingers itch to stroke him. I'm sitting cross-legged at his hip and allow myself to visually inventory every hill and valley of his body.

"Why were you naked?" I wonder as I watch the firelight play across his skin, or rather, his scales.

Gently touching his wrist, I smooth my fingers along his scales, enjoying the texture. It's not slimy like some people think. It's dry and slightly pebbled—interesting to touch.

My gaze travels to his hairless head. I won't lie, ever since we discovered their race and their interest in a mating compact between our species, I imagined what it would feel like to trace my fingers along the patterns I would find there.

This Draal's markings, the appealing dark and light blue stipples, are so interesting compared to my pale tan skin. I wonder if he'll find the smattering of freckles on my cheeks as interesting as I find his colored variations.

His lips are thin. I've imagined kissing lips like that almost every night since the first pictures of Draalians filled my newsfeed.

And his nose, almost non-existent, intrigues me as well. As my eyes sweep down his body, I decide this male is a perfect specimen.

I've tried to keep things professional, but I can't control myself from inspecting more closely. Down wide, powerful shoulders to perfect washboard abs, to trim hips, to slightly jutting hip bones that make my mouth dry. But my gaze dips lower to the main attraction. Or attractions as it were.

I realize my hand is still braced on his shin, keeping his knee bent from when I was applying a clean bandage. I guess the back of my mind had this visual inspection in mind all along. His cocks are on full display.

I'm no expert on cocks. There hasn't been a male born on this planet in ninety years—not one that lived, anyway. When I look at porn, it's certainly not flaccid cocks I'm interested in. So what I see is more interesting than arousing.

They call the top one their secondary, the bottom one is primary. I can only imagine what they'd look like erect. Well, I can do more than imagine. Although I've only had it a short time, I'm well acquainted with my Draalian sexbot.

I wish I could say it was a waste of money, but it wasn't. It was worth every penny. I don't know if I'll ever be able to afford a real mate, and the automated one has given me a lot of pleasure.

In addition to the two cocks they're noted for, I see the bumps and ridges described in the literature as well. Although it's state of the art, whoever designed my sexbot didn't do this race justice —these masculine shafts beckon me.

I force myself to quit staring and tear my gaze back up his body toward his face, but can't contain myself from saying, "I wonder what you'll look like when you're awake. I bet you'll be magnificent."

Blood is already seeping through the bandage. Shit! I need to take it off and treat his wound again.

Zoriss

Searing pain in my thigh. Warm hands on my shin and wrist.

I lie quietly, eyes closed, keeping my breathing still and calm. Where am I, what is going on, and why does it feel like the flames of hell are licking at my groin?

It's quiet and smells musty. The hands on me are small and warm. Her scent is female. I can't detect if anyone else is in the room, but I'll bide my time until I figure out what is going on.

"I wonder what you'll look like when you're awake. I bet you'll be magnificent."

My translator works. I understand her perfectly, but the language doesn't sound familiar. Zorn and I have been fighting . . . where were we stationed last? I can't recall. Weren't we due for furlough? The last thing I remember is . . . the last clear memory I have is saving Zorn's life on planet Pythian. Somehow, that doesn't seem right.

The female's hands move to my groin. I have to force myself to keep my eyes closed in order to maintain the element of surprise, but is she about to harm me? To inflict more pain?

Are we alone here? I can't sense anyone but her, and I need to find out if she is friend or foe. Her touch is gentle, but the pain is severe.

I don't care how many others might be in this room, I'm a lieutenant in the Draalian planetary army, I can't lie here helplessly forever.

My eyes snap open and I grip both her wrists so tightly she gasps in pain as her blue eyes pop open wide, looking at me for what, mercy? Sitting up, I wince as every muscle in my body protests, but I focus on my task—subdue the female and conduct recon on my situation.

She's a warmblood—a mammal. Humanoid. No species I've seen before. Are we in a cave? I keep a tight hold on her while I glance around. I see no others.

What planet is this where they live in caves lit by fire?

"Where am I?" my voice sounds gravelly as if I haven't spoken in weeks. I sound like this when I wake from a long stasis.

"Crap," she says. "My translator must be malfunctioning."

Perhaps the populated areas are advanced and there are rural areas with cave dwellers. What else would explain a female in a cave mentioning a translator?

"Who else is here?" I continue to scan the environment, looking for others of her kind.

She looks up at me with pleading eyes. "I don't understand you."

"Who else?" I shake her, my eyes blazing so she knows I'm not playing.

"I . . . my translator doesn't work. I don't have much use for it out here. I had no idea it was broken." Her blue gaze is full of fear and holds no aggression.

Tightening my grip, I look around. We're definitely in a cave, and by the look of things, we're alone.

"What do you want with me?" I bite out.

She looks at me helplessly and shakes her head, obviously having no idea what I want.

I inspect her now, taking her measure. I haven't known many females, just family—my mother and aunts. Our female population had been declining for a century, but the disparity between males and females spiked in the last generation. I've never known a female my age.

This one is soft. And scared. Her pulse is hammering under my fingertips. In one sweeping glance, I inventory her bland, colorless face, the symmetry of her nose, and the blonde hair on her head and browridges. Although she's not an attractive species, her face is interesting. Perhaps over time she would appear pleasing to the eye.

"What were you doing to me?" I ask in Draalian, knowing she can't comprehend a word of it. Looking down at my lap I see a gash high on my right thigh. I'm no medic, but it's close to my femoral artery. I want to accuse her of doing this, but it's jagged and obviously wasn't performed with a knife.

I examine the cave. "Are there others of my kind? Like me?" I ask. "Where's my brother? My platoon?" I gesture to my chest, although with no translator there's little chance she could possibly understand me.

"Draals?" she asks.

She knows my race.

"Draals." I nod.

"Just one," she says, indicating one finger, then pointing it at me.

I point behind my right ear and tell her, "I understand you."

"You understand me?"

"Yes." She's smart; she catches on quickly.

My head throbs. I release one of her wrists and explore a spot above my brow that's pulsing in pain. It's swollen, tender, and when I pull my fingers back they're specked with dried blood. I have a head injury. That explains both the loss of consciousness and memory problems.

"Y-you're hurt. I was tending to you," her voice is a whisper, her eyes luminous and terrified. "Your head has already stopped bleeding, but I need to close your wound." She glances at my lap.

I nod at her, giving her permission to do so.

"Lie back?"

I shake my head, I'm not putting myself in a vulnerable position. I still don't know who she is, what she wants, or if more of her tribe will be joining us soon.

She tries to pull away, but I shake my head.

"I need supplies. In the pack." She motions with her head toward the pack to her left. I nod, releasing her left wrist and tightening my grip on her right.

24

"See?" she says as she shows me supplies. "I was going to wait to close your wound until I was certain it wasn't infected, but it won't quit bleeding. Here." She lifts a small tube and shows it to me. "This will close the wound."

"Go ahead." I nod.

She's sitting on the cold stone at my side, but because I won't lie down, she has to scoot back, bending low to get access to the injured area. I release her wrist, but grab the waistband of her pants to keep her from escaping, although she seems to have no desire to run as she works on me.

"I'm a vet. A veterinarian. Oh," she glances nervously at me, then back to her task, "not that I was implying you're an animal. Sorry. It's just that I don't want you to worry about your medical care. I know how to use medi-seal."

Her fingers are warm. I've never had occasion to touch a warm-blood before. Her touch is light, I'd almost call it tender, as she works on me.

"You're on Earth, of course you must know that, in the River of No Return Wilderness. It's a two-hour hike almost straight down to get here. More like three or four hours to climb up. That's when you're in good condition. Which, of course, you're not." She pulls on both sides of the wound, readying it for the sealant.

In that position, her hands and head are inches from my cocks. I'd have to be dead not to respond. Both cocks are now straining for attention, vying for space in the crowded area of my lap.

"Um . . ." She looks up at me, embarrassed. "Maybe with your other hand you could . . ." her gaze flicks toward them.

For a moment, I consider not complying as I wonder what it would be like to have a feminine hand touch me there at least once in my life. I may not have known any females my age, but I was raised by a mother who taught Zorn and me how to be decent Draals. I push my cocks out of her way and try to focus on her efforts instead of her proximity.

Her breath caresses me as her face turns in that direction. One hand keeps the wound pressed together as she works with the medi-glue.

"I hiked down to save a moose, a calf, even though it's not a good time to be down here. There are no guarantees a blizzard won't hit us and then we'd have a hell of a time climbing out. I just felt compelled to save the little fellow.

"I was looking for him when I heard this high, whooshing noise. Your one-person vessel was a fireball when it came down, and then there was the most spectacular crash."

I'd wondered if perhaps my platoon was nearby, but she's describing a one-person vessel. What would I be doing in that? Is it an escape capsule? What was my unit doing here? Why was I in an escape capsule? Is my brother Zorn okay? Why am I here?

Her nimble fingers are trying to close the wound, which is a job that would be difficult under the best circumstances. Now, in the firelight, with me sitting instead of lying down, and my cocks happily bobbing inches from her face, it is *not* the best of circumstances.

A lock of her hair brushes against my primary. Why this gentle brush of silk feels more sensual than when I fist myself, I have no idea.

"I thought it was an old satellite crashing to Earth. It happens sometimes. These things are relics. Who knows why they're held up in the sky one moment and fall the next? But I ran toward it anyway for some unknown reason."

Aunt Madreen does this same thing. When she's nervous or uncomfortable she talks too much—a constant stream of meaningless chatter.

If this female's planet has satellites and medi-glue, what is she doing in a cave? Did they have some cataclysm and revert back to prehistoric ways?

"So I came running, and the capsule door popped open and there you were. I knew immediately you were a Draalian. Well, yeah, that was obvious."

Her hair brushes my primary again and it returns the favor by pulsing toward her.

"Uh . . ." She clears her throat, bends closer to her task, and applies the medi-glue to one side of my scales, then closes the wound and holds it for a minute.

"I think that will do it," her voice is deeper, obviously relieved as she sits up and tries to back away.

I'm still holding her by her waistband, so I just shake my head and spear her with a burning look. I don't know why I won't allow her to scoot away, it's not that I fear she'll hurt me. Actually, I do know why I'm keeping her close. I like her proximity.

I inhale deeply and ignore the musty damp smell of the cave, focusing instead on the flowery scent of her hair. The hair that a moment ago caressed my primary. In my lifetime, this is the closest I've been to a female my age. Now that I don't fear interruption by her tribe, all I can focus on is wondering what her breasts would feel like cupped in my hands. No, not just that.

My brain pounds with the even more urgent question of what she might taste like.

Perhaps I can't read her species' nonverbal cues, but I don't believe she's interested in me. She's stuffing her medical supplies into her bag. With each precise movement, I can feel her trying to inch away. Her fear of me is palpable, so I release her. She immediately scoots back and eyes me as if she's afraid I'm going to pounce on her.

I'm about to ask where the rest of her people are, but she won't understand the question. My eyes can answer it anyway. She's obviously alone here. Other than rocks, the only things I see are her two blankets, the sleeping bag I'm sitting on, one pack, and a metal disk holding firewood. I don't think I have to worry about her tribe returning to harm me.

"So . . . it's pitch dark and well past my bedtime." She laughs nervously as she leans away from me. "I'll just steal one of these blankets and bed down over there." She points across the fire.

I shake my head and grab her ankle, not wanting her to leave me helpless and unattended. If I let her go, will she leave me alone in this cave? Although I try to lie to myself about her possibly wanting to abandon or harm me, I can't deny she just willingly patched me up as efficiently as a Draalian field medic.

Through trembling lips she says, "You understand me, right? On Earth we have an old saying . . . no means no. You probably have that on your world, too. I mean, that's just the civilized way to do things. So, uh, I'm saying no. Perhaps you're wondering what I mean, like no to what. Well, no to anything but me taking one of your blankets, going to the other side of the fire, and sleeping without being molested."

We're alone together and she's terrified.

"I won't hurt you," I say, trying to look non-threatening, although I don't know how a large reptilian male can appear non-threatening to a small mammalian female. I take special care to cover my fangs with my lips.

Now that I don't think the males of her tribe are on their way to kill me and I believe I'll live through the night, I pay attention to other urgent matters. Like the fact that it's cold here.

I test the air with my tongue and believe even with the fire, the temperature is dangerously cold. We have two blankets for two people. How can she live in a cave with no fur pelts?

I don't know how to explain it to her, but I won't make it through the night with only one blanket. I'll need to share them both. And I'll need her body heat.

The sleeping bag I'm on is short but at least most of my body is partially protected from the cold stone. I pull her toward me, share the unzipped open sleeping bag with her, place her between me and the stone wall of the cave with the fire at our feet, and cover us both with the blankets. I grab the disc with the wood and yank it closer, then toss a few more logs on the fire.

"Too bad you can't understand me, Earther. You'd know I mean you no harm." I tried to say it softly, with as few 's' sounds as I could, so my hissing didn't scare her.

Since I can't communicate with words, I pull her down and nestle my front to her back. Despite the fact that I'm trying to reassure the female I'm not going to harm her, my cocks haven't received the message yet. They're rock hard and get even harder when they're pressed against the back of her thighs.

"Please don't. You have to know this isn't right." Her tone is half command, half plea.

If this was my frightened little nephew back on Draal, I would stroke his head to reassure him, but it's a terrified Earth female and I don't think my touch will comfort her in any way.

She's trembling. It must be from fear because she's at least twenty degrees warmer than me. I'm freezing. I pull her even closer, trying to share her body heat. She struggles to pull away, but I croon to her, trying to calm her.

"It's okay, little Earther. I mean you no harm," I say in the lilting singsong that Draalians use to lull their babes to sleep. "You'll be fine. We'll just go to sleep and wake up, Tomorrow will be a good day."

I'm in an interesting position, being with a female is fascinating in and of itself, but being able to say anything, knowing she doesn't understand a word is a unique opportunity. I decide to take advantage of it.

Lifting up on an elbow, I peer over her blonde hair to see her face. "Your flat face is interesting."

Her eyes flare wide, showing white all around the blue. I'm not calming her. After tightening my arm around her waist, which pulls a startled "Oh" from her, I give in to my impulse to sing a few of the songs my aunt sang to my nephew when he was in her arms. This soothes her, and finally she settles down.

Lumina

I've never been this scared. Ever. I read about human history. I know about rape. It happened in every culture, every level of alleged civilization. As much as I've longed for male companionship my entire life, I knew things weren't all unicorns and rainbows when men walked the Earth.

I've fantasized about a Draalian for years, ever since we agreed to be trade partners. His government approved the trade and many of its citizens were excited to come here.

Interested people of his race go through screenings—psychological, physical, and emotional. If approved, and if they are still interested, they immigrate here on vessels and are housed in nice facilities until they pick a woman who also chooses them.

I researched every aspect of this, even picked the matchmaking company I want to use. I just never had enough credits for the fee.

All these years I've dreamed of being in an embrace just like this one. But I never imagined I'd be sharing a blanket in a cave with no way to communicate.

His cocks, so beautiful when he was unconscious, are pulsing menacingly against the back of my thighs. As much as I wanted to be a sexual female with a mate, I never wanted to be taken against my will.

Whatever comes next is going to hurt. I can't say I've never been penetrated before. I've played with sex toys; it's commonly accepted in our culture.

But I have a feeling what he's going to do will be nothing like I'd imagined my first time with a real male would be.

I always thought of myself as a strong woman, but I can't control the silent tears sliding down my face, or the sob that quietly escapes my sealed lips.

He scoots away from me and nudges me to roll toward him. We're still only inches away from each other, only now I'm facing him. He tips his head as he inspects my face. He's looking at my tears. I try to dash them off my cheeks but he stops me.

He says something. It sounds like a question. His voice is deep and rumbly. In different circumstances, I'd consider it sexy. Right now, though, I'm so terrified even the two cocks pulsing near my sex aren't erotic.

He looks interested, fascinated actually, by my tears. His head tips as he captures one with his index finger and inspects it. His nostrils flare as he inhales its scent.

I'm mere inches from him and have a front-row seat to the action. Every muscle in my body clenches when that forked blue tongue presses between his lips and delicately tastes the teardrop.

Once I read an article titled, "We're Just Apes Wearing Clothes." It reminded the reader that no matter how you dress us up, we're still animals. Well, the animal in me just responded to the animal in him. There was something so supremely sensual about that little action that I can't control the zing of arousal flying through my body like a manic fairy godmother lighting things on fire with her wand.

How can I be terrified and aroused at the same time? Not only does it sound insane, it doesn't sound smart in an evolutionary sense.

His head cocks toward me, as if the fact that I'm crying baffles him.

"Tears," I explain, hoping he'll stay focused on the drop on his fingertip and not the smell of my arousal in this cave. I read that Draals have a keen sense of smell—especially for *this* smell. "We cry when we're sad or scared. You wanting to have sex with me without my agreement makes me hurts my feelings.

"I should probably remind you that I climbed into the canyon, ran to pull you from a capsule that looked like it was going to explode at any moment, pulled you to safety, dragged you a mile along the riverbank to provide you shelter, built you a fire, and tended to your wounds. I deserve to be treated with a modicum of respect and released from my bonds, but at the very least . . ." I have to grab a breath of air, "you shouldn't rape me."

His head snaps back even as he begins to shake it. "No. No," he says, then pulls away as far as he can while staying under the covers.

His hands come up between us in the classic 'don't shoot' pose.

"No means no," he says, as he gazes solemnly at me.

He heard me when I said that earlier! He even committed it to memory. In English. I heave a long breath through pursed lips and feel every cell in my body stand down.

His blue eyes are beautiful and so sincere. They're the most 'human' thing on his body, and they're speaking volumes to me, urging me to trust him.

He must feel my muscles relax, because he leans closer and this time he doesn't use his finger as a middleman. He cautiously licks my cheek, setting off a tremor of seismic proportions that rocks me to my toes. Why this is more erotic than the cocks still pulsing against my belly, I'll never understand. Maybe because it's exquisitely tender, or it's so unexpected, or maybe because even my two-thousand credit sexbot didn't have one of these.

He murmurs to me now. His voice is a sexy combination of masculine rumble and dangerous hiss. But the look on his face is . . . concerned.

"I'm sleepy. I should really get to sleep," I say in a rush.

He reaches up and grazes his knuckles along my cheek in a caress as soft as a whisper. After a few more quietly husked words, he scoots as far away as he can while staying under the warmth of the covers, and then turns away.

It takes me long minutes to truly believe he's going to leave me alone and go to sleep, but I'm beginning to believe he means me no harm.

~.~

I must have overcome my fear and drifted to sleep, because I'm abruptly awakened. My body morphs from fast asleep to full-on panic in the span of a second. It takes me a moment to fully awaken and remember where I am—and why.

Okay, I'm in a cave in the middle of the night sharing blankets with a Draalian. But why is he burrowing into my body? His face is pressed to my throat, one leg is slung over mine and pulling me close, and both hands are under my t-shirt, fingers splayed across my back.

Yet there is nothing sexual about this. Nothing. The penises that were prominently pulsing against my belly last night are nowhere to be seen—or felt.

"What's wrong?" Stupid question. Well, any question is stupid when you can't understand a word the other person says.

Now that my brain is back online, I sort the problem out quickly enough. It's freezing in here. Looking past the fire, I see snow lightly drifting down outside the cave opening. The stone underneath us, separated from us by a thin sleeping bag, is unrelentingly cold, and the blankets covering us provide little in the way of warmth. And he's naked.

He must have already added more logs to the fire, but it's a large cave with a high vaulted roof, and the heat dissipates quickly into the frigid air.

"Cold?" I ask.

He pulls his face from the shelter of my neck long enough to give me a nod.

Draalians are humanoids. They walk on two legs and are at least as smart as humans. But they're aliens—*reptilian* aliens.

Reptiles are called cold-blooded for a reason. They have no ability to regulate their temperature. They can't shiver when they're cold in order to warm up. When they get cold enough for long enough, they go into torpor. Their systems shut down, they quit eating and drinking and eventually they quit moving and die.

I consider for a moment. I have a change of clothes in my pack. Had I not been so terrified I couldn't think, I would have offered them to him earlier. At least my t-shirt, the pants would never fit. But even if he could wear my clothes, they won't provide near the amount of warmth my body can.

I debate with myself for a few seconds, knowing the alien male could misinterpret what I'm about to do, but really, what choice do I have? I push him away long enough to pull off my t-shirt and jeans, having taken off my bra and leather gaiters before I went to sleep.

"This is not a sexual invitation," I say as I climb on top of him and pull the blankets over both of us.

Our gazes lock, my face an inch from his. I have a front-row seat as I watch his expressions change from shock to relief. His shuttered eyelids and the soft sigh he releases tell me he must have immediately received some benefit from my body heat.

A satisfied rumble escapes the back of his throat as his shoulders relax.

He says one word. Out of all the millions of words in his language, I'm pretty certain he just thanked me.

His arms surround my back, they're cold as ice. He reevaluates and sneaks them between us, palms down so he doesn't cop a feel. Just squished in there so they can feel my heat, too.

He's murmuring now. The words are soft. By the gentle look on his face, I think he's reciting a litany of thanks.

Zoriss

Her behavior makes no sense. She's scared to death of me, thought I would rape her, she even cried. She said that signified extreme unhappiness.

So why would she tear off her clothes to warm me? It's an act of generosity. Other than my mother and Zorn, I've never experienced generosity to this extent. I like this female.

She's watching me as closely as I'm watching her. At least I know some of what floats through her mind. She seems incapable of keeping her thoughts to herself. She knows nothing of me, though.

"Zoriss," I say. "My name is Zoriss." I move my hand to point to my chest and accidentally graze the tip of her breast with the back of my hand. She sucks in a surprised breath as her eyes flash open. "Sorry," I tell her and look down in apology.

"Did you apologize? Did that word mean 'sorry'?"

I nod.

"Zoriss? That's your name?" She chooses not to mention my inappropriate touch.

I nod.

"Lumina. My name is Lumina."

"Pretty name," I say, although I know she doesn't understand. Earlier tonight I realized I could do anything I want to this female. I'm so much bigger and stronger than her, I could . . . force things. Rape, though, isn't allowed on my planet. It's abhorrent. I could never, *would* never, cross that line, even with an enemy.

Remembering that I can say anything with impunity, I ask, "Why are you doing this? You think I'm capable of rape, you have to know the position you've put yourself in would tempt even the most honorable male. And from what you know of me, you couldn't be certain I'm honorable. Why?"

Her head is angled as she pierces me with her gaze and shakes her head clearly not having a clue as to what I'm asking

I tuck her head against my chest, both for warmth and to keep her intelligent eyes from gleaning too much information.

It's quiet.

We don't have snow on Draal, but I saw it once on planet Pythian. My brother and I were in the same platoon. He got separated from us. Through our psychic link, I knew he was hurt, dying. My captain forbade me to search for him, but I snuck out to find him . . . or his body.

I thought I would die that night—many times. It was desperately cold, colder than it is now, but I had layers of clothes, including my thick uniform coat. It hung to my knees and kept me warm, but it was stark crimson against the white snow. It was a miracle the enemy didn't spot me.

I found Zorn dying in a puddle of his own blood. Enemy fire had nicked his carotid artery. Ironic that the cold which almost killed him slowed the bleeding and put him into torpor. I carried him back and our medics healed him. We always had a strong bond, stronger than most clutchmates, but this bound us together even more tightly.

We have a psychic link, but I can't reach him. I pray he's safe. If he's alive, he's probably looking for me right now.

We're a good pair, he and I. I'm more of a doer, he's a thinker. He scolds me for being impulsive, I chide him for being too analytical. I wish he was here now. Together we'd figure out how to find our platoon and get out of here. If he's alive, he's looking for me right now.

On Pythian, I found that the blanket of snow creates a hush. It's the same here. All I hear is the snapping and popping logs, and Lumina's breathing.

The back of my hand feels as if it was burned along the line where it grazed her nipple. The thought pops into my head that when I'm ninety I'll still remember the exact path her nipple trailed oh so many years ago back in that cave on Earth.

Right now, I feel their two pebbled points press against my chest. My cocks hardened the moment my body began to warm. How could I blame them? They're nestled against her belly, her soft skin covers mine. I feel her quick, warm puffs of breath dance across my skin.

I'm warmer now. Truth be told, although I'm still chilled, I wouldn't go into torpor if I let her roll off me right now. But I don't want her to.

Her muscles aren't rigid anymore. The longer we've lain like this, the more relaxed they've become. Since my hand already left the warmth it found when it was wedged between our bodies, I might as well put it to good use. I stroke her hair.

Draals don't have hair. I've stroked household pets before, but never anything like this. Her yellow hair feels like silken springs. It's fun to touch—and arousing. I wait for her to protest.

"Tell me to stop. If you want." It's not a very generous offer, since she has no idea what I said.

For once she's quiet, so I proceed. Just this gentle stroking of her curls. My cocks kick at the joy of this, the intimacy. She pretends she doesn't notice them pulsing against her belly.

"I've never been with a female," I say into the quiet air. It was unnecessary. Not only can't she understand a word I say, but if she knows about Draals, she also knows there are no available females on our planet. The few that are born are placed into arranged marriages before their first birthday and they're cloistered after that.

Cocking my head, I observe her face from an angle. What I see highlights our differences. She has eyebrows instead of browridges. Pale eyelashes fan her cheeks. And her nose can be seen in profile where all I have is a slight bump. Could I get used to this, I wonder. Could I ever find her attractive?

The blood pulsing through my cocks tells me I already do.

The Earther is quiet, which doesn't bode well. Earlier tonight she chirped constantly; I decided it was anxiety. But her silence? I wonder if that's somehow worse.

"Why are you quiet, Lumina?"

"I don't understand what's going on," she says as if she understood my question. "This situation is so . . . unexpected."

She's right. The situation is odd. I don't know how I got to this planet, where my platoon is, or what my mission is, but perhaps this circumstance is a stroke of luck. She risked her safety to rescue me from the capsule, then brought me to the cave, treated my injury, and is now lying here like this—to warm me.

I allow my hand to stroke lower, as it leaves the safety of toying with her curls and touches the skin on her back.

"You're freezing," I say as I tuck the blanket more securely around her shoulders. Instead of tightening at this small incursion, her muscles relax.

"You like my touch." My announcement shocks me. How could she? She was terrified a few hours ago, but she seems to have calmed as we've lain together.

I become bolder. My palm sweeps past shoulder blades, down her backbone, skirts her ribs, and lodges at the small of her back.

When one finger slips below her waist, she says, "Uh . . ." This is her eloquent announcement that I've gone too far.

"Point taken," I tell her as I inch my hand away from the invisible boundary.

It takes only a moment for her muscles to slacken again. My fingers and palm explore the rectangle of her back—up and down, side to side. Too close to the swell of her breasts on either side garners me another, "Uh." Otherwise, she's content to let me pet her.

"Are you beginning to trust me, Lumina? I'd like that." My voice sounds deep to my ears, perhaps too loud in this quiet space.

As if to confirm that I was correct about her appreciating my touch, her little tan hand moves from where it was lodged at my side and rests on my pec.

This one touch, almost innocent, sets off a tremor throughout my body. I wish I could contain it, but it's a reflex.

Growing up on Draal, knowing the dire problems our global warming caused, the severe shortage of female clutches, I knew with certainty I would never have the opportunity to enjoy the touch of a female. To have this now, innocent as it may be, floods me with emotion.

"I like it when you touch me, Lumina," I croon.

She lifts her head to look at me, her blue eyes inspecting me closely as her other hand moves between us mirroring the first to gently rest on my pec.

I show her my emotion and let my lids close. I don't even try to hide my deep sigh.

When she lifts her torso higher to look at me more closely, her pebbled nipples drag against me. I shudder, accompanied by a noise that erupts from the back of my throat. It's a cross between a groan and a hiss.

"Are you warm enough, Zoriss?" Her pretty head is cocked as she awaits my answer as if it's of the utmost importance. Did I just think of her as pretty? Obviously, I'm finding her more attractive with every passing minute.

Do I tell her the truth? Will I nod my head only to have her roll off of me and show me her back as she did earlier?

Despite my desire to the contrary, though, I *am* an honorable male. I tell the truth—always. Reluctantly, I nod my head.

The tiniest smile lifts the corners of her lips and instead of rolling away, she straddles me, her chest still pressed to mine, but her knees are now digging into the sleeping bag under my hips.

I swallow and let my gaze drink her in. Did I think she was bland and unattractive only hours ago? She is the very definition of beauty.

Her rounded breasts, the pink nipples hard and begging to be held in my palms. Her pouty lips, her springy curls, the swell of her hips. I could look at her all day. But I won't.

She's given me an invitation, the least I can do is give her reassurance in return.

"No means no, Lumina," I say in her language having heard it earlier. "I understand."

Now a true smile lights her face. My mission is accomplished. I've set her worries to rest.

Lumina

You'd never know it by looking at me, but I'm waging a war inside my head. A very intelligent part of me is waving a red flag and has turned my internal klaxons onto their loudest setting. They're warning me to stand down. Immediately.

The other part of me is determined to follow my body's desires. I've dreamed of having a mate, a husband, a lover, since I got my first period. No, it was way before that when I had childish dreams of walking down an aisle and then holding a man's hand and kissing with clothes on. And for the past five years, I've dreamed of having a male who looks just like the one I'm straddling.

My slit has been dripping wet since his skin began to warm. Even before that, since those searing blue eyes looked at me with appreciation when I was tending his wounds. And his hand, stroking my back as sweetly as I would pet a kitten? I feel like I died and went to heaven.

I wonder if it was fate that I wound up here in the canyon at the exact moment the Draalian needed me. What else would it be? But it doesn't matter. I'm here. He's here. And I'm not going to let this opportunity go to waste.

I don't care how many cautionary thoughts are pulsing through my brain. The desire to experience this, even if it's just this one time, overrides them all. He's not just handsome and sexy, he's been nice, respectful. For once in my life, I don't want to do the smart thing, the levelheaded thing. I want to give in to my desires.

I don't know how brazen I should be. I'm a strong female, a doctor, but in my fantasies it was always the man who took the lead.

"You're handsome, Zoriss." This is the first male I've met in my lifetime. We're skin to skin and his hard cocks are pulsing against my belly. I have no idea how to flirt much less have sex, and we've known each other a grand total of a few hours. But I've waited a lifetime for this, and I want to explore the attraction growing between us.

His gaze locks onto mine and he speaks several sentences. His eyes are so sincere, and his words are soft and hypnotic. He knows I can't understand a word he's saying, but he keeps talking, gentling me, crooning in his foreign language full of sibilant hisses.

"I wish I understood," I confess.

He presses his palm to my cheek and strokes me with the softest touch imaginable. A small smile lifts the corners of his mouth. Smart male, he's decided to speak with his body instead of his mouth.

I feel safe with him, although I don't know why. Actually, I do. His naked flesh is smashed to mine, his cocks have been standing at attention for a long time. Despite his injuries, he could have hurt me in a dozen different ways a hundred different times because he's so much stronger than me. He's done none of that. He seems content to simply stroke my cheek.

His thumb rubs my bottom lip. It's a simple action, a soft brush. I've touched myself here a thousand times in my life. But it's never felt like this. It's sensual, almost magical.

He has to know it's turning me on, doesn't he? My nipples, drawn to hard points since I tore off my clothes and climbed on top of him, could drill rock. And my scent. Surely he can smell my arousal wafting through the cave.

He keeps brushing, though, just the gentle touch back and forth. A stream of words flows from those sexy Draalian lips. I have no idea what they're saying, but I make up a script. He's telling me how pretty I am, how sexy my body is, how much he wants me. Is he telling me how he laid in bed alone on his planet dreaming of me as I dreamed of him?

Whatever he's saying is sweet, because it has to match the look of interest and adoration in his compassionate gaze.

"I'm attracted to you, Zoriss," I confess, having no desire or need to hold back my thoughts. I flash him an open smile.

He smiles back. Holy shit. The Draalian is so handsome when a smile lights his face. Those blazing blue eyes, the color of a butane flame, sparkle. They look right at me as if they can read my mind. And his fangs! I've dreamed for years of fangs like that scraping the mounds of my breasts.

He slides his palm down the column of my throat, then explores my collar bones. I've had this body for twenty-eight years, but it feels like I just dropped into it and am experiencing it for the first time.

I've wanted many things in my life. From childhood toys to going to vet school, to wanting a Draalian. But I've never wanted like *this*. Never desired like *this*. It strikes me that because of the language barrier my Draalian is going slow. He can't talk to reassure me, so he's telling me with his soft touch how much he likes me and how respectful and gentle he can be.

I realize I don't want slow, or gentle. I want passion, and I want it now! I could tell him, I guess. He understands me, but I don't want to tell him. I'll show him instead.

"Should we do this, Zoriss?" I roll off and quickly remove my soaked panties, then roll back onto his body. I spread my knees farther apart and slide up a single inch knowing I'm coating his belly with my cream.

He releases a stream of rapid-fire words, his wide blue eyes asking questions I'll never comprehend.

"No means no, Draalian, but yes means yes." I hold his gaze, hold my ground. I'll not allow myself to retreat now.

To make sure my point isn't lost, I grab his wrists and place his hands on my breasts. The moment my nipples are resting in his palms, I throw my head back with a hiss of pleasure.

He likes my noise, and returns a hiss of his own. All of a sudden it hits me, and a bolt of fear travels up my spine. I'm really doing this. I'm going to have sex with an alien from another planet. An alien I've never even had a conversation with.

His long, strong fingers pluck both my nipples at the same moment and all thoughts of bolting and running and protesting leave my mind. In fact, *all* thoughts leave my mind. I just want to sink into this experience and enjoy whatever comes next.

He scoots my ass up and pulls my shoulders down so my right breast falls into his mouth. We both hum with pleasure at the same moment.

His tongue, that facile, blue, forked tongue, goes to work on the hardened nub sending me to the stratosphere and back. My eyes fly open wide because the level of pleasure is shocking.

"Zoriss!" I gasp, noticing this drew his attention. To leave absolutely no doubt that the noise was breathed in pleasure and not pain, I say, "So good. Don't stop."

His hands lodge on my ass cheeks and he presses me closer as he pulses his hips against me, maneuvering me so my slit slides against his primary. This pulls a deep, surprised moan from me.

The war I was having moments ago? The one where I was deciding if I should go forward with this or not? That's ancient history. Now the war I'm having is whether I should just bask in this pleasure, or if I should somehow slip out of this embrace and grip his cock. Oh, and should it be just one, or both of them?

I decide to do that later, as my mouth pops open in a little 'o' of pleasure when he mimics what he's doing with his tongue on one nipple with his fingers on the other.

"Too good," I say as encouragement to ensure he doesn't break his rhythm.

I grab his shoulders and throw my head back as I thrust my breasts out in offering, arching my back. He continues to work one nipple with his tongue and mouth and lips while his fingers pluck and strum the other.

When I play with myself at home, I don't spend much time with my breasts, I'm usually focused on physical release and have developed techniques to get me there in record time. Now, though, I want this to go on forever. It's building exquisite pleasure inside me, causing desire to swirl in my pelvis.

My fingers dig into his muscular shoulders, feeling the pebbled texture of his patterned blue scales.

Lifting his head to press his mouth near my ear, he releases a torrent of words. Although I have no idea what he's saying, I believe I get the general idea. Strings of words and phrases and sentences and paragraphs. By the tender, passionate tone of his voice, I can only imagine the sexy praises and promises tripping off that lovely forked blue tongue of his.

Dipping my head so he can relax and let his head lie on the sleeping bag, I bombard his ear with my own string of words.

"You're so sexy, Zoriss. Look at you, your body is like a sculpture. Every muscle, every hard plane and chiseled ridge is in perfect proportion." My tongue darts into the tiny shell of his ear and he sucks in a loud gasp of pleasure, his eyes flaring wide at the sensual surprise.

With his obvious approval of my touch, I roll to his side and grip his secondary cock in my palm, the one closest to his belly. A string of gritty words flies from his lips as his lids shutter closed. Although I can't understand Draalian, I doubt he's telling me no.

"Fuck," I say, having no other words to describe what it's like to have his stiff, hot cock in my hand. Stroking from base to tip, I revel in the ability to make it pulse in appreciation.

When he says "No," my eyes fly to his, wondering why he's the one who wants to shut this down. He rolls me onto my back and slips his knees between mine.

He's not ending our game prematurely. In fact, I think he's trying to ensure I don't bring him to completion when the party's just getting started.

He's on hands and knees, his head dipped to the inside of my knee as he nips and licks and lips his way up my thigh. The visual of this huge, magnificent alien, naked except for his glinting silver armband, bent in the service of pleasuring me is almost more arousing than the act itself.

As he makes his way northward, he lifts his head from time to time to say things. I supply my own subtitles, "You taste so good," I imagine he's saying, or "I can't wait to savor your come on my tongue."

"Me, too."

He laughs, then hovers over my clit, just breathing on it while he inspects my face, waiting, perhaps for me to say no.

"Waiting for me to beg, Draalian?" I ask as I catch his eye.

The slowest smile spreads across his face showing his white fangs in all their dangerous glory as he nods once with unhurried precision.

"What if I refuse?" I challenge for no discernable reason.

He sits up, his ass resting on his heels, his smile broadening as he waits.

"Are you sure this is your first time, Zoriss?" I ask, assuming a male with almost no females on his planet has never done this before. "You seem pretty sure of yourself."

For some reason this makes him decide to rescind his demand for my pleas, because he moves fast as a blur and presses his mouth to my clit.

I hiss in pleasure.

His tongue, rather than being the blunt instrument of some of the sex toys I've tried in the past, is dextrous, facile, and delicious. The two halves come together to put pressure all around the little ball of nerves as he does recon, exploring the lay of the land. Then his tongue splits, flicking on both sides of my clit until I wonder if I will be able to live through the onslaught.

"Zoriss." How interesting that his name is a hiss.

His large hands grip my upper thighs and yank me open wider as he shoulders himself even closer to me. One knuckle trails up and down along my feminine seam, sliding through my juices, amping me up even more.

"Please," I say. It's the only word I can articulate, even though I don't want him to have the satisfaction of hearing me beg. He's male enough not to gloat, though. He doesn't break his rhythm.

His knuckle now presses into my core, just an inch, maybe less.

"Oh, yes!"

He takes this as an invitation and slides one finger inside me. Certainly he knows what this is doing to me as I toss my head from side to side in pleasure.

It's amazing I haven't come already. Between the relentless flicking of his tongue, the rhythmic penetration, and the visual stimulation of the male of my dreams kneeling in front of me, I'm already on the precipice.

He must know I'm close. He speeds up his tongue, somehow adding an animalistic hiss that jolts through my system, zings up my body, and lodges in the pleasure center of my brain.

My orgasm whips through me, circling and amplifying and gathering power instead of dissipating. I can't turn off my poor brain when it tries to calculate whether that was one long incredible release or maybe three or four short, back-to-back ones.

I scream at myself inside my head to shut the fuck up even as I scream the word "Fuck," out loud so intense and so long the echo resounds and reverberates around the cavern and over our heads.

Before I open my eyes, I worry the Draalian is going to have a smug look on his face and I try to prepare myself for it. When I see his handsome features, though, there's nothing smug about it.

I imagine he's looking at me the way I looked at that doe so many years ago. It was a combination of wonder and privilege that she allowed me to get so close.

The words rolling off his tongue are a sexy combination of honey with a side of hiss. When he finally stops talking and sits back on his heels to gaze at me I have to prompt. "Tell me more."

He laughs, but there's no derision in his expression, then launches into another Draalian soliloquy. When he finally grinds to a halt, I flick my gaze to the two cocks pointing eagerly at me and ask, "So what's the plan of attack?" I tip my head and cock an eyebrow.

"No means no?" he asks, one browridge cocked in query.

"Yes means yes, Draalian."

When he bestows that smile on me, I feel privileged.

He sits with his legs crossed and pulls me with his hands under my armpits to sit on his lap. Then he positions me with my knees near his hips. Somehow, we manage to avoid even a brush against his wound. His hands slide to my hips, steadying me, yet providing no pressure, as if to say, "Your move."

Not only am I still aroused as hell and curious about what's to come next, but I like this male. He's pleasant and passionate and concerned about pleasing me. He's handling his injuries and this odd situation so well. When I get a working translator, I want to know everything he said to me in this cave. I want to fuck him. And I want it now.

I feel desperate to climb onto him, and shy as that doe at the same time.

"Just one for now, right?" I ask. I haven't even gotten a good look at his primary cock, but from the shadowy outline I saw, it looked as big, possibly bigger, than the first, which is impressive in its own right.

"One." He nods.

When I lift myself, he grips my ass cheeks and helps me ease down. My lids flutter closed as I dive deep into myself so I can feel every inch of this invasion. Is it an invasion if I impale myself, I wonder, then scold my crazy brain and order it to stop the commentary and just live in this moment.

Oh yeah. This scaled blue cock easing into me makes my inner walls flutter.

"So big," I say as I take a breath and exhale through pursed lips.

The large bulge halfway down the shaft that I saw before he woke up poses a small problem. At first, I'm certain it will never fit, and I'm not sure I want it to. A nanosecond later, though, I'm desperate to keep pressing down, and a moment after that the stretch and burn feels sexier than anything I ever could have imagined.

I release a throaty noise of appreciation as I take the widest part of his patterned blue girth inside me, then slide farther down.

His head is thrown back. I see his Adam's apple thrust toward me and watch it bounce as he husks something in his language. I'm certain it means something like, "So tight."

I force my eyes to open as my rubbery lips ask, "Good for you?"

A long stream of satisfied words later, he nods.

Easing down in increments, I notice every interesting ridge created by the patchwork of his scales and the intriguing bumps and ridges that are common to his species.

"Full," I tell him, feeling compelled to give my own commentary.

He embraces me now. His hands leave my ass and wrap around my back. There's a sense of overwhelm with his proximity and alienness and the huge cock in my core and his other one bobbing against my back hole. It's almost too much, but then nothing can be too much when it feels as good as this.

I reach bottom and stop, still as a statue, just basking in the exquisite feeling of having a living, breathing Draalian male inside me, filling my most private places.

He thrusts up, proving I hadn't yet fully reached bottom at all. He gained another inch, maybe more.

"Zoriss." I'm swamped with warm feelings for this male, and those beautiful blue eyes are so tenderly looking at me.

"Lumina," he husks.

He feels it, too.

His palms return to my hips as they gently urge me to start my ride. As I lift up, he presses forward, ensuring the drag of my clit along his pelvic bone on every rise and fall. It doesn't take me long for the already volcanic pressure in my core to build to incendiary heights. I could come with just one word from him, but I wait.

His breath hitches, and he can't control himself from thrusting in response to my movements. I allow myself to ease back, counting on him to guarantee we don't separate.

Good male, he kept us connected. Now that I'm lying on my back, it's me who's urging him on. "Ride me, Draalian. Fuck me."

He responds immediately, as if he was only waiting for me to say the word. He pounds into me, creating a swifter, harder, more primitive rhythm than I'd initiated. He releases a little hiss with every thrust. I answer with a shocked intake of breath every time, as if I both can't believe it's happening and can't believe this act could provide the exquisite pleasure I'm experiencing.

I wanted to wait for us to orgasm together. I've read about it and watched it on vids and dreamed about it. But I can't wait. I fall into the chasm, letting go and wailing in ecstasy. I feel my inner walls clamping down on his hard cock, even as I hear a woman screaming and realize it's me.

I think it's my response that pushes him over the edge. I watch as his face tightens, grimacing in an ecstasy that matches my own. He shouts a word, certainly a curse word that signifies his physical bliss. His teeth scrape my shoulder. If I'm not mistaken, he almost bit me with those two small, sharp fangs that peek out between his lips sometimes.

He lies on his side and pulls me against him. His expression is soft, almost sweet for a reptilian.

I'm sweating, but I realize he's probably still cold, so I reach around him, grab the blankets we kicked off in our passion and tuck them around him. I won't need them for another minute, not until my heart quits racing.

"Too bad that was so disappointing," I tease.

He nods and smiles at me as his fingers feather through my hair.

Zoriss

I wish I could talk to my beautiful Earther. I want to tell her that was as far from disappointing as it could be. I want her to hear my praise and gratitude in her language.

"That was amazing. Exceeded expectations. So much better than anything I could have dreamed of, Zoriss."

I grab her wrist, realizing we haven't kissed. Perhaps I could start with her hand.

I kiss the center of her palm with my lips, then flick it with my tongue.

"Holy shit, Zoriss. That felt like you licked my . . ."

She looks shocked.

"You have no idea how many times I imagined what it would feel like to do what we just did. I began thinking about it the moment the first pictures and vids of Draalians hit our airwaves. The government approved an exchange of your people to come here as mates, and I knew I wanted one of you. Not the other species. A Draalian. Only a Draalian"

Is she talking about me as if I was a species of canine she wanted to own? Am I hearing correctly?

"I began saving credits then and there."

She's been saving? To *buy* me?

Without warning, everything comes tumbling back into my brain. Going back to Draal on furlough with Zorn after five years of fighting our enemies. I remembered wrong. I'm not a lieutenant, I'm a captain in the Draalian army.

Three long months in that pod. How could I forget that? Three months with nothing but my own thoughts looping endlessly until I began to wish for death.

How could I forget the voices of the pirates talking about the evil Earthers who wanted us for nothing other than our cocks and our sperm?

And my vow to take revenge? I can't forget that.

The Earther must be anxious after our physical exchange because her words are tumbling out in torrents.

"Everyone in town knows how much I want a Draalian. They all ask me how my savings account is coming. I do odd jobs just to be able to afford a mate. I'll be honest, I never thought I'd get there, though. The prices are so high. It's unattainable for most women in my income bracket."

Unattainable except for the black market. Just pay a pirate and they can steal you a first-rate captain in the Draalian army. She may not be the female who actually purchased me, but she is just as guilty since she condones this behavior. It fills me with shock and rage to hear she was saving credits to buy a mate even if it wasn't me.

Hate bubbles up inside me. Rage. I have more loathing for this female than I did for my enemies, the Vrens.

"What are the odds? Really? I can't even calculate the astronomical odds of being here at the bottom of this canyon the exact moment your capsule crashed. And you were alive!"

She looks at me, her eyes dewy with excitement. Half of me wants to make her pay, pay for every female of her race who condones abducting sentient beings and bringing them here against their will. The other half of me is waiting to hear the next shit that will fall out of her mouth.

"And here we are, and you are so . . . magnificent. I can't believe how lucky I am." She's beaming. She used that word earlier to describe my cocks.

I'm not flattered, I'm furious. I'm an object she admires and desires. I feel tricked, betrayed, and used.

If I wasn't an honorable male, I would make Lumina pay. Right this minute. It's not my nature to physically hurt a female. That's beneath me. But I can hurt her with my words. Even if she doesn't understand them.

"You are an evil female," I spit at her, hoping she fully comprehends the extent of my hatred. "Earth females don't deserve mates if they believe it's their right to buy us, willing or not, like a pet. Despicable." This word in Draalian is 'shamispah'. I allow the 's' to form an angry hiss to communicate how truly despicable I find her.

I grab the rope webbing from the metal disc and tie it around her wrist, the wrist of the hand I was just kissing, and I yank it tight. If I didn't have good self-control, I would be doing this around her throat.

Lumina

"Ow! That hurts!"

Instead of loosening it, he cinches it tighter.

"What just happened? Zoriss, what did I say? Your translator must have malfunctioned. I said you were magnificent. That's a good thing."

If I didn't know for certain that his eyes couldn't shoot fireballs, I'd be afraid of bursting into flames.

I don't know what he's saying, but he's hissing at me, looking as if he's restraining himself from hurting me.

"Zoriss! You were just inside me. We exchanged bodily fluids. You looked into my eyes as if you had tender feelings for me. I . . . I was just joking about it being disappointing. Is that what set you off?"

He's grumbling now, shaking his head. Even though the gray fingers of dawn are lighting the sky outside our cave, he lies back down to sleep.

"Really?" I ask when he pulls my back to his front in order to garner my warmth, as if it's his *right*. "You're going to treat me like shit and then steal my warmth? Fucker!"

"Fucker!" he snarls next to my ear. Out of all the English he hasn't learned, he has to pick up on that word?

Even though he can smell my tears and I try to forbid myself from showing weakness, I can't stop them from falling. How can a person experience the height of bliss and ten minutes later crash to the depths of despair? I wish I could disappear.

Lumina

I'm rudely awakened by a yank on my tether. Looking up, I see him scowling furiously as he attempts to change his own bandage. His legs are sprawled open and his head is dipped low as he tries to tend to his wound while keeping hold of the binding that keeps me next to him.

I took some psychobabble personality profile test years ago, before I applied for vet school, but I didn't need the results of some bullshit test to tell me what I'd known since I was little— I'm a helper. I donate too much to charity, I give away too many services for free in my practice, and I'm a soft touch in general. Hell, that's the reason I hiked into the River of No Return Wilderness. I just want to help.

So it's no big surprise when I have the fiercest urge to help the asshole sitting next to me. It takes all the strength I have to sit and watch him struggle. If I was a mean person, I'd jiggle the arm that's tethered to him at the most inopportune time. But I control myself.

And if he wasn't the world's largest asshat, he would ask for help. But no, he just scowls as he struggles with what's now his third attempt.

Finally, "You're going to waste all the supplies. Here." I grab the wrap, wrench his thighs open wider, and inspect.

It's hard to tell, the guy's got scales instead of skin; he's blue instead of any shade of human skin, but I wonder if this is getting infected. After straining to reach my pack, I rummage for the antiseptic spray, give him a liberal dose, then bandage him.

He grunts at me. It's a no-eye-contact monosyllable.

"I'll take that as a warm thank you. You're oh-so-not welcome." Prick. I still have no idea what caused his abrupt change in mood. I feel angry and hurt and used and most of all, vulnerable. And the change from the warm connection we shared to him shutting me out? Right after we both had our first sexual experience? That was the unkindest cut of all.

He stands and moves toward the fire, now so close it's a good thing he's hairless, or he would singe his body hair.

I kneel next to my pack, dump the contents onto the blanket, and take inventory.

"My empty water bottle, package of water purification tablets, ten nutrition bars, one and a quarter rolls of bandage, half a can of antiseptic spray, two pairs of panties, two t-shirts, a pair of jeans." At the bottom is a hoodie, I don't know why I forgot it was smashed in there.

"Here." I tap him with it, not wanting to risk throwing it into the fire.

"Uh." He sees what it is, then looks over his shoulder at me, eyes wide in surprise. He knows I'm freezing, too. He grabs it, quickly unties the cord on his wrist and puts it on in one swift movement. At least he doesn't re-tie the rope.

"Don't mention it," I say when I realize not even a terse thank you is on its way.

Then he says it, the word I think is a Draalian thank you. It's so belated and so grudging I can't take a modicum of joy from it.

"I have no idea when we're going to be able to climb out. We need to ration the food. How hungry are you?"

Reptiles only need to eat sporadically. The ones on our planet can go five to seven days or longer without a meal. I don't know how this works with Draals, nor do I know when he last ate.

He shakes his head, a clear indication he's not hungry, but the way his eyes dart to the food, I wonder if he's lying.

"You're already debilitated. You're injured and freezing. Think you should eat?"

He shakes his head again, then lifts his chin toward the food, indicating I should eat.

"I'll wait," I tell him. "We both need to drink." I fill the collapsible pot with fresh snow from the entrance to the cave and set it near the fire to melt, tossing in a purification tablet.

The day passes slowly as Zoriss casts longing looks out the cave opening. It snows from time to time without a lot of accumulation. I imagine it's the lack of heat and sunlight that bothers him the most.

"Looks like no basking for you today," I state the obvious.

He gives me his first direct glance of the day. It's mournful.

I'm sitting on the sleeping bag with both blankets pulled over my shoulders. The bag does little to cushion my ass from the hard stone floor, nor does it keep the cold from seeping into my bones.

What makes me more miserable is watching him. He's sitting directly in front of me at the fire. The hoodie covers him from the waist up. From the waist down he's naked, hugging his knees.

"Oh, I forgot," I say as I walk to the back wall and retrieve the stuff I grabbed from the capsule after I rescued him.

I inspect what I thought might be a med kit, but it's basically bandaids and medications so far past their date of expiration they're either dust or dried into cement.

"Is this food?" I ask with a grimace after looking at the little packages I wondered were freeze-dried insects.

"Mmm." His eyes light up with interest.

"Have at them." I hand him the packages. The pictures on them look like crickets and mealworms.

He grabs them, divides them into two equal piles, and hands me half.

"Really? Generous, but no thanks." My stomach does a slow, rolling dive.

He cocks an eyebrow. His expression looks as if he's baffled by my lack of interest.

"They'll taste like ass. They're all yours."

He stashes them with his half of the bars, opens one as if it's a Godiva truffle, and savors every crunchy bite.

I try to stifle my disgusted shiver, but don't succeed.

It's barely after noon and I've thought about what happened last night a thousand times. Five hundred of those times were about what occurred before he switched personalities. They were pictures of the sex we had, the physical bliss, and the tender look in his eyes.

Five hundred were replays of what happened after I told him he was magnificent. The blazing anger in his eyes, the harsh words he spat at me.

"*Shamispah*," I say, unable to imbue it with the level of hatred he did last night. "Wonder what that means." I'm baiting him. I know it. I have no idea why I don't even try to contain my urge to ruffle his already-ruffled reptilian feathers.

This catches his attention, more even than the hoodie I handed him. His eyes shoot me fireballs.

"I have an idea. Let's play a game. I'll teach you English so you can communicate with me. I'm pretty smart. I bet I know just what words you'd like to add to your vocabulary."

He turns to give me his full attention, arms across his chest, cocks flaccid.

"Bitch. It means a spiteful female. Or it can be a verb that means to complain. Say it," I taunt, daring him not to play.

"Bitch." His face looks bland.

"Come on, Zoriss. You can do better than that. Say it with feeling."

"Bitch!" is said with enthusiasm as he warms to our little game.

"What's the Draalian word for that? One you'd use for a male?" I ask, my eyebrow lifted. I'll learn a few appropriate words to communicate, too. "On Earth that word is bastard. Bastard," I repeat, diving into the spirit of the game.

"*Chareen.*"

"*Chareen.* That has a nice bite to it. Let's see, what next? Fuck you. 'Fuck' is what we did last night. It's sex without meaning." That jibe was so accurate a stab of pain pierces me as I admit it out loud. "'Fuck you' means I don't like you, go to hell, eat shit and die. It's used for someone who you deem despicable."

"*Shamispah,*" he says as he pegs me with the coldest gaze I've ever received.

"No. Fuck you."

"*Shamispah.* Despicable."

"That's what that means?"

He nods slowly, as if talking to a child, or an animal, to make certain I get the full extent of his hatred. "*Shamisssspah.*" There, he adds that wonderful fillip of the hiss to make certain his meaning is clear.

"You find me despicable, Draalian? How about a male who fucks a girl and then insults her? How *shamissssssssssspah* is that?" He thinks he can hiss? Well I can fucking hiss too.

"*Shamispah,*" he admits with a nod, although he shows no evidence of contrition. He's not sorry he said it.

"*Chareen,*" I taunt as I turn my back to him and face the rear wall.

And that, boys and girls, ends our little vocabulary lesson for the day. I can add *chareen* to asshole, bastard, and prick as his list of identifiers.

Zoriss

I thought lying in a pod for three months with my body unable to move and my mind unable to rest was hell. That was a vacation compared to this. Being trapped in a primitive cave with a despicable female who believes in slavery, one who was saving up to *buy* me like I'm a pedigreed canine? Fuck her. I like that Earth word. Yes. Fuck her.

I'm freezing. That doesn't help. During drills in military training, we learned how to stand all day without fatigue. But I'm not in military training. I'm on a strange, cold planet. I've been unable to bask, haven't had anything other than liquid nutrition and one tiny *minten* since I left Draal, and I lost a great deal of blood.

I had already cleaned my wound before Lumina woke up this morning. It had seeped through and bled profusely on the blanket during the night. I was blissfully unaware of my wound when I was deep inside of her but I am painfully aware of it now. She's a doctor. I know she should look at it, but it was all I could do to allow her to bandage it. I'm surprised, though, that she hasn't discovered the spot on the blanket where I bled.

After our verbal sparring match, I give in to my body's demands and lie down. The nutrition bars are still neatly stacked in two piles. She didn't have to share with me. She'd have every right to hoard them. And she saved my life. I can't deny that.

I shove the bars into the pack and stow it near the cave wall. She's right, we need to ration. I'll wait until I'm hungrier. Which means weaker.

Perhaps tomorrow the sun will shine and I can bask a bit then hike up the side of the steep canyon. Then what? Will more Earth females attack me? Bid on me? Force me to mate with them? I know nothing of the rules here.

~.~

I fell asleep and slept hard. It's dark outside and the fire is blazing. Lumina must have crawled over me to get to the wood and stoked the fire without disturbing me. I'm logy, my thoughts sluggish, possibly approaching torpor.

She's sleeping as far from me as the blanket will allow.

My traitorous mind flashes me reminders of how warm I was with her last night. Between her delicious body heat and her plush body, it was as if there was a furnace burning inside me, warming me from within, just like warmbloods must feel every minute of every day.

I've been in torpor before. On planet Pythian after I saved Zorn's life, I couldn't get warm. Luckily our platoon was there. They nursed us back to health. Would Lumina? Would Lumina nurse me back to health if I slipped into torpor? My eyes dip in shame when I realize I wouldn't if I were her. I'd let me die. She finds me as despicable as I find her.

I need her warmth and, assuming she won't offer it, I need to take it.

After pulling off the hoodie and t-shirt she loaned me, I slide behind her, tuck the blanket around us, and slip my hands under her shirt along her back. It's all I can do to stifle my moan of relief. Her skin is like a heater. My hands are like ice.

When she doesn't rouse, I gently pull her shirt up as far as I can without waking her and snuggle against her. My chest rides her back, my hands splay across her belly.

I don't like her. She taught me the right words earlier today. I find her a bitch and want to tell her 'fuck you'.

I'd be lying, though, if I said I didn't want to fuck her. My cocks should be the last place in my body that my brain allocates its precious supply of blood. But my mind must be addled—my two engorged cocks are a firm testament to the fact that a great deal of my blood supply has been sent south of my waist.

"What?" In one second, Lumina went from deeply asleep to wide awake and full of anger. Her voice is deep and growly as she says, "You can't just take what you want, Zoriss. You can't touch me without my permission."

Right, but you condone stealing me from my planet and selling me to the highest bidder. Hypocrite.

"Roll over. Go to your side of the bed," she demands.

How do I communicate that I can't? If I do, I'll die. She's an animal doctor. She has to understand this.

I nudge her to get her to roll toward me, then grab her palm and place it on my forehead. Her eyes flare open. She understands.

"You're too cold," she says. It's not a question.

I nod.

"You need my heat."

I nod solemnly.

"Okay. This time there will be rules. Break a rule and I won't help you again. Got it?"

I nod.

"From here to here?" She indicates the top and bottom of her breasts. "That's the no-go zone."

I nod.

"My panties? No-go."

I continue to nod.

"Nothing sexual, Zoriss. Nothing. Say okay."

"Okay."

After she pulls off her t-shirt and pants and presents her back to me, I scoot next to her and can't suppress my moan of pleasure at being so close to her internal furnace.

My cocks are hard as metal against her thighs. As despicable as *I* find her, *they're* enamored. I vow to keep them under control tonight.

Lumina

I'm no herpetologist, but I went through a reptile rotation and have treated pet frogs, snakes, and chameleons in my career. Zoriss is far too cold. I couldn't say no to his request to use my body heat, although his request could have been a bit more courteous.

There isn't an inch of space between us. Even his cheek is pressed against my neck, trying to garner a bit of warmth there.

But it's the cocks drumming against the backs of my thighs that gather my attention. I can picture them, pulsing and blue, against my pale flesh. Although I try to shove that thought out of my mind, it just hangs there, flashing like a neon sign. *Traitor,* I accuse myself.

My nipples prick into hard points, aching to feel the press of his palms which are only inches away.

I try to command my body to stand down even as I feel my core lubricating, readying itself for a delicious invasion like it experienced last night.

His body stiffens as he sniffs once. Although it wasn't accompanied by words, it's as if he just spoke a paragraph of condescension, criticism, and contempt.

"I can't help it, you know. I'm sure you can smell me. It's a reflex reaction. Don't act so high and mighty, Draalian. It's not as though I can't feel not one but two cocks hammering against my thighs."

He grunts in acknowledgment.

My nipples ache for his attention, my core is desperate to be filled again. My mind flashes me pictures of last night, hinting how much it wants a replay.

I have an internal debate, but it doesn't last long. I admit to myself that if he asked, I'd agree in a heartbeat. I'm not proud of it, but it's true. One thing I won't do, however, is ask for it. That's a line I will not cross.

It's so quiet in here. Just the snapping fire and our breathing. He's not asleep, his breathing is too rapid and his body is too fidgety. And those cocks. I don't think a male could go to sleep with his cocks pulsing so hard.

I read once that the old technique of deciding something by coin toss proved only one thing. When the coin was flipped and in the air, you discovered what you really wanted by paying attention to what you wished for.

If I tossed a coin right now, what would I wish for? It wouldn't be for him to fall asleep right now. No, I'd want his hand to start ranging up and down the front of my body. From one 'no-go zone' to another.

Zoriss

There are those on my planet who deny evolution, but I don't. I know Draalians advanced from lesser animals, but I hate when those vestigial aspects of myself make themselves known.

Like right this moment. My animalistic self is craving the female whose body is pressed to every inch of my front.

My face is lodged against her neck, her springy curls tickling my neck. Instead of irritating me, I find it arousing. My hands are splayed on her belly and itch to violate her no-go zones.

Her scent is powerful. She's emitting her arousal as though there's a bellows between her legs specifically designed to beckon me.

What harm would it do to replay what we did last night? Her body signals its readiness. Mine is certainly willing and able.

Would I be a traitor to my race, to my very principles if I partake of the bounty set before me? Or would I be following in the footsteps of every marauding army from days of yore who took the spoils of war?

This is war, I make no secret of it. After all I've been through, those months on that vessel, paralyzed and in mental agony. Don't I deserve to quench my need in her channel?

I'd never force her. Never. But if she's willing? So am I.

My hand rubs her abdomen, not just staying within the lines she delineated but respecting large margins. I avoid the forbidden zones by inches.

Her muscles tighten for a moment, then I feel her relax. I've just begun my plan of attack, but her reaction tells me I've all but won the war.

Her breathing is louder, faster. Her scent bursts in the frigid air of the dim cave. I won't violate her boundaries, though. I have to wait for an invitation. Even *I* am not that *shamispah*.

I lick the fragile column of her neck, then flick my tongue into the shell of her fascinating human ear just as she did to me yesterday. It affects her mightily as she gasps in surprised pleasure. I breathe in through my nose, ignoring the blatant smell of her arousal, focusing instead on the smell of her breath and skin.

Her hips thrust almost imperceptibly. I'm certain she didn't want me to catch the movement, but I did. It signals her interest. Her mind might not want me, but her body does.

My respectful assault continues for long minutes as I ramp up her arousal. She's squirming under my hands as I keep them compliantly within her designated lines. I'm a captain in the planetary army. I vow to outwait her. She has to ask.

Finally, after wiggling against my cocks and writhing to trick me into palming her breast, all to no avail, she breaks the silence.

"I changed my mind, Draalian. Touch me however you wish."

Lumina

It's been two days since we began our uneasy truce.

I hate him even more than I did the night he called me despicable, because he makes me feel like a fucking addict. An addict who would do anything for their drug of choice. My drug of choice just happens to be a big, blue Draalian.

I gave up all pretense of self-respect that night when I invited him to cross my self-imposed boundaries. When he indicates a readiness to be with me, I never say no. It's not just that, though. Half the time I don't wait for him to approach me, I approach him.

I have to give him credit, he quit being mean. I haven't heard the *shamispah* word once since we attacked each other under cover of darkness. I wonder if he loathes himself for his weakness as much as I do.

Things are strained to the breaking point between us. He's actually been polite—overly polite—never failing to offer me half the cricket-things he eats when he's starving. I'm unfailingly nice as well, controlling my urge to tell him I hope he chokes on them and he's almost as gross as they are.

We engage in that tense civility you give to your worst enemy in high school when the teacher is watching. Where your lips say all the right things while your eyes promise you'll be enemies forever. I can't wait for him to be healthy enough to climb out of here.

I hate him and desire him in equal measure. Even though he walks around in a hoodie and a ridiculous blanket fashioned toga-style, I still can't tear my eyes from him. The feeling's mutual, too. I feel his gaze on me when I stoke the fire or leave the cave to relieve myself.

He untethered me that first day. Somehow he knows I won't leave him until he's healthy enough to climb out. He walks to the mouth of the cave and watches me when I leave for a moment, though. He doesn't completely trust me.

I scavenge for firewood and collect water one small collapsible pot at a time. He's still too debilitated to do any heavy lifting.

For the first time since we arrived, the sun shines outside. We've had nothing but snow showers for days, but today it's warming up and I definitely see sun out there.

"Basking will help you, right?" He's looked gray for days, and is getting weaker. Last night even our sex didn't last as long as it usually does. That was a clear indication his health is worse.

He nods.

"We're down to one nutrition bar. We both know you're slipping into torpor. No amount of my body heat . . ." I don't mention the "or sex," I assume we're both thinking. "No amount of my body heat will make you better. I think you should bask as long as you can this morning. We need to finish that bar and then climb out. I think if we wait any longer, we'll both be too weak to make it."

"Yes," he says. He uses one of his few English words.

He removes his toga and hoodie and lies on a large flat rock a couple hundred feet away on the riverbank.

Naked Draalian. I've studiously avoided thinking of him as *my* naked Draalian. He's made no secret he finds me both sexually desirable and *shamispah*. The moment we get to the top of the canyon, I'll find a way to contact the authorities, get him to a Newcomer dormitory and we'll bid each other a not-so-fond adieu.

Around noon, he stands, wipes his hands, and returns to the cave where I've packed everything but our last bar.

I've got on my t-shirt and jeans as well as the hiking boots I arrived in. He looks like something from a post-apocalyptic movie. In addition to his hoodie and blue-blanket cape, the gaiters I loaned him sit atop rags from the blanket we cut into strips and tied around his feet. And of course, his cocks are waggling in the wind.

"Here you are." I hand him half of our last bar.

We've been savoring our tiny meals until now, but today, we just scarf the food down. He holds out his hand, offering to carry the pack, but at this point I think I'm stronger than him, so I slip it on and we set off.

The path is full of sharp rocks and brambles. I imagine by the time we get to the top of the canyon that rags or no rags, the soles of his feet are going to be cut to ribbons. Oh well, there's nothing either of us can do about that.

I've never claimed to be in good shape. I'm not a fan of treadmills or running or lifting weights, but I lead the way. When I glance over my shoulder from time to time, it's clear he's struggling.

Basking this morning made him less gray and more blue, but it didn't make him healthy.

We're a little past halfway when I see spots of blue blood flecking the trail behind us. He's bled right through his blanket-shoes.

"How about we rest, Zoriss? Let me re-tie your shoes."

When he willingly sits down and doesn't grumble or argue, I know how much the climb has taken out of him.

"I know this is hard, but we're almost there. As soon as we get to the top, I'll get you into my vehicle and turn on the heat. I have a couple of blankets in the blizzard box in the back. You'll be warm for the first time in days."

Both of us sneak a side glance at each other when I mention that. We know that's a lie. When we're fucking, he doesn't seem to mind the cold. I don't say that, though.

He's still breathing heavily, so I keep talking to let him get ready for the steep climb ahead.

Zoriss

"I'll get you to the authorities—"

"No!" What's already happened isn't bad enough? Does she want to torture me more? Terrible visions fly through my mind of being strapped on a gurney and forced to ejaculate to feed these Earth females' endless desire for Draalian sperm. Or being strapped to a bed to be a pleasure slave for the greedy female who bought me. Why would Lumina threaten me with such things?

"Of course I'll get you to the authorities, Zoriss. How else do you think you're going to get off this planet? I'll get you to the officials and they'll put you in a facility for newcomers. I think there's one a couple hundred miles from here."

"NO!" Facility for newcomers? Is that what they call the hell-holes they'll lock me up in? I'm a strong male, but how can I overcome all the power the authorities can bring to bear? My eyes round in fear at the threat.

"The government regulates these places. They are desperate to repopulate the species, even if it means using alien DNA to make it happen. They advertised on your homeworld, they've made it attractive for you to come."

Attractive? So they can lure us here to use us?

"You'll have your own room. I hear they're lovely. The Draals are given the sunniest rooms with large basking rocks. If you choose to stay, they'll help you learn a craft or trade so you can become an even more valued member of our society. Only if you want, though."

Valued member of society?

"What do you mean? I wouldn't be tied to a bed? Forced to perform? I'd be treated . . . nicely?" I still sound panicked and desperate.

"You know I don't understand you, Zoriss, but something's not translating correctly. Let me start at the beginning. You hit your head, is that the reason for the miscommunication? Do you not remember why you're here?"

"Tell me more. Explain from the beginning." I give her my full attention so she knows I want to hear her.

"After you decided you wanted a mate from Earth, you took tests. We don't accept just anyone. The authorities must have deemed you worthy. You had to be mentally, physically, and psychologically fit. Then we brought you here, free of charge, and taught you basics about our language, culture, and society along the way.

"I don't know why you were in that capsule, or where in the process things went haywire for you, but when you got here, you were supposed to be transported to one of our facilities. There you were to be welcomed, shown your room, and introduced to other Draals who came before you.

"You were supposed to receive even more education and then begin making your selection of a mate from a list of those interested in you."

"My selection?" I'm shocked. I was supposed to be given training that was to be helpful, not just to help me function better as a slave? I was to be allowed to find a female who appealed to me? I was supposed to be given choices?

"We value you so much, Earth women pay a great deal of money to be included in the process. Between the vetting on your planet, the free trip here, the facilities where you're housed and fed, the intensive testing of both males and females to make certain we're compatible, it comes to a large expense."

Does this explain why she was saving her money?

"Earth females who are interested have to shoulder some of the financial burden by paying fees to the mating agencies. I think I mentioned earlier that I hadn't yet made enough money to buy into the program yet."

I look at her in shock—my eyes wide and my jaw open. All the things that haven't made sense since I met her now click into place with thunderous clarity.

She wasn't trying to buy me, she was saving to pay the agency for the chance for someone like *me* to pick *her*.

She's been kind and caring from the start. How could I not see the reality of the situation?

I continued to believe what those fucking pirates told me, the line about cocks and sperm, rather than the flesh and blood female who shared my bed. The one who was kind and generous and put up with my despicable behavior. The one who not only saved my life, but kept me from going into torpor by sacrificing her own comfort. And I called *her shamispah.*

I shake my head, so angry at myself for my unforgivable behavior I want the soil to swallow me. Look at her. She's beautiful. And kind. She tore her clothes off to warm me, to save my life, and I treated her with contempt. How do I apologize for that?

Apologize? That would never be enough. How do I repay her for all she's done for me?

My gaze probes hers as I wish for the thousandth time she had a functioning translator. It's my fondest wish she could hear my heartfelt apology.

I scoot closer and touch her cheek with exquisite softness. She doesn't understand my words, perhaps she can comprehend my touch, the look in my eyes.

I gather her in my arms and pull her onto my lap, ignoring the pain when I accidentally drag her across my wound. I just hold her tight and croon.

When she pulls back to examine my face, I try to explain with the few Earth words I know.

"Lumina. Sorry. Sorry. Sorry."

I rock us both side to side. "Sorry. Sorry. Zorriss *shamispah*."

Does she understand me? I kiss her neck, her cheek, her nose, her forehead. I try to make the kisses as nonsexual as I can. I don't want her to think this is about coupling. I want her to know this is about my change of heart and my sincerest apologies. These aren't the desperate, sensual, provocative kisses we usually share. They're sweet. Caring.

I grab her chin between my thumb and fingers and tip her head so she can look into my eyes. Perhaps she can read my expression. I command my features to display kindness and compassion and so much contrition.

"Your generosity humbles me. I was so harsh to you and you never failed to be kind. How can I ever repay you? How can I ever apologize enough?"

"Are you apologizing?"

"Yes, yes, yes. Sorry." I nod emphatically.

"For being mean?"

I nod, never veering my gaze from hers.

"You misunderstood something?"

I nod.

"It's cleared up now?"

"Yes, Lumina. Yes."

Her muscles slacken and she leans her head on my shoulder.

"I don't think I even admitted to myself how hard these last days were on me. You were so mean," her voice sounds so sad.

I was. How can she bear to even look at me?

"Zoriss sorry."

Tears spill from her eyes. Perhaps she's allowing herself to release the emotions she's held inside since the first time I told her how despicable she was.

I put one finger under the lovely point of her chin, tip her head toward me, and lick her tears from her cheeks, just as I did our first night together.

"Sorry," I say in a soft, heartfelt whisper.

I'm the stupidest male in the galaxy. Here I've been in enforced intimacy with a beautiful female whose fondest dream was to save enough money to legally mate a willing Draalian male. She so clearly wanted me. She's obviously a good person who risked her safety to drag me from the capsule and haul me back to shelter.

She could have hiked out of this canyon days ago, but she didn't. To help me. I was too weak to get my own water from the river. She shared her food with me.

And how did I repay her kindness? How many times did I call her despicable? How many ways did I try to communicate how little I valued her? And how many times did I take advantage of how generously she shared her body heat with me, despite knowing how much I disliked her?

And allowing me to sheath myself in her? How many times did she allow me inside the private warmth of her body? And how many times did I thank her? I don't know the answer to any of those questions, except the last. The answer to that is none. I never let her know how much I valued her generosity. How spectacular it was to be allowed to bring her pleasure.

"Thank you, Lumina. Thank you a thousand times. If you can find it in your heart to forgive me I promise I will make this up to you."

Look at her. This female who has every right to hate me is looking at me with trust.

"I haven't earned your trust, pretty human, but I will. I swear I will do whatever is in my power to make up for every hurtful word and glance."

I stand, feeling stronger now that things are cleared between us.

Reaching out my hand, I say, "Let's get to your vehicle. I want you to get a translator so you can hear every word of the apology I owe you."

"You're ready?" she asks.

I nod.

"You don't hate me anymore?"

"Sorry," I say in her language, hoping the earnest expression on my face conveys my sincerity.

She retrieves her gloves from where she laid them on her pack, then embarks up the ravine. It's so steep at this point we have to cling to the side of the wall, grasping shrubs so we don't tumble down.

I don't even see what caused it, but all of a sudden Lumina topples past me with a sharp cry of fright and lands in a crumpled heap twenty feet below me. When I see her lifeless body, my heart squeezes in my chest.

I scramble after her, my knees pistoning, taking the impact so I can race faster. Is she dead? She's not moving. Placing my fingers on her carotid, I feel a pulse, but she's unconscious.

My energy was flagging. I was close to torpor before we began the ascent, and could feel myself weakening as the climb progressed. But clearing things up between us gives me strength. And now, knowing she needs me, I'm energized.

My hands skim along her limbs as I check to see what's broken. Nothing, although she must have hit her head.

I carefully lift her and heave her over my shoulder. She makes a little moan, but I don't have time to soothe her. I scramble at my fastest speed to traverse the rough terrain.

One hand clutches her legs to my torso, the other grasps anything I can hold onto as I pull myself up the steep canyon. Even though I'm low on energy, I spare what little I have to talk to her.

"I'm going to get you help, Lumina. How can I ever repay you for your sweetness and generosity? I'll do anything I can to show you how repentant I am for the way I treated you. Just wake up."

I slip, losing my foothold and sliding at least ten feet back down. All I can think of as time slows and I experience every bump and jolt is how not to lose my hold on the female in my arms and how to protect her if I fall.

I come to a skidding stop, still on my feet, and immediately charge upward again.

"I'm going to make all of this up to you," I vow.

When I'm only a few feet from the top, I have to use both hands to pull myself up as I balance her on my shoulder. Eventually, I'm standing on flat ground, gasping for breath, swaying with fatigue, Lumina held in both my arms.

There are three vehicles in the lot. I don't know which is hers. Even if I did, I wouldn't know how to operate it or where to take her.

I've been in battle against our enemies before—many times—yet I've never experienced panic. But I'm panicking now. My heart pounds and fear circles in my belly. Lumina needs immediate medical attention and I'm powerless to make that happen.

She called this a wilderness area. What if these vehicles are abandoned, or if their owners are going to be hiking in the canyon for another week?

It's obvious Lumina has a concussion but I don't see any signs of civilization from here, and odds aren't good that I could carry her very far. Torpor and exhaustion are setting in.

I hear gravel crunching behind me and whip around to see what danger is hurtling at us now. It's a female in hiking gear, a large brown canine on a leash by her side. The female's eyes and mouth open in fear as she looks at me.

I know I look odd in my blue cape and rag shoes. Lumina, comatose in my arms, probably doesn't give this female confidence, either.

"Help," I say, assuming she won't understand me, but hoping she hears the desperation in my voice.

"Hiking injury?" She doesn't approach, but doesn't run from me, either.

"Lumina fell. She must have hit her head." Does this female understand me?

"Hurry. Climb in my vehicle and I'll rush you to the hospital."

If I was alone, I would debate with myself about trusting this Earther. Except for Lumina, I still believe all Earth females only want my cock and my sperm. But I force those worries down and follow her. Lumina needs help.

The back seat is like a bench, so I gently set her on it, then slide in and place her head on my lap. I only now realize that my cocks are hanging out. No wonder the female is as leery of me as I am of her.

"I'm Skye, this is Poochie," she says as she starts the vehicle. "I'll get you to the nearest hospital."

I take in the scenery as I watch it fly by. From what I've seen of it, Earth is a pretty planet. I just don't trust its inhabitants.

It feels like an eternity before we arrive. Skye comm'd ahead, and there are two hover-stretchers waiting for us at the hospital doors.

After thanking Skye, I tell the staffers I don't need a stretcher when they approach the vehicle.

"Honey," an older female with blazing red hair says, "if you could see yourself right now, you wouldn't argue. You look like death warmed over. Get on the stretcher. It's not a request."

Her hand is on her hip and she looks to be all business. For some reason, I don't get the impression she means me any harm. I do what she says after I watch them gently ease Lumina onto her own stretcher.

When they rush us in two different directions, my anxiety rises.

"Don't worry, honey. We're going to take care of her. You both get your own team. You're stuck with me. You're my first Draalian, but I've studied up. How long since you basked?"

"This morning, but not for long."

"You climbed up from the river in the canyon? How long were you there?"

"Six days."

"You eat regularly?"

I shake my head. "We were low on food. I crash-landed. Lumina rescued me."

They transfer me onto a heated bed, then cover me with a thin heated silver blanket that wraps me in a cocoon of warmth. For the first time since I landed on this forsaken planet, I'm not cold. I only realize now that a moment ago I actually moaned in pleasure.

They ask for our demographic information. I tell them I'm too new to Earth to know much more than my own name.

As two staff wash me, I resent their proximity as the smell of their arousal blooms on the air. Their bodies may be interested, but their hands are all business. While they're performing their duties, the red-haired doctor examines my wound.

"Your companion attended to your wound?"

I nod. I don't know what to say, not wanting to get Lumina into trouble.

"She did an excellent job. I'm going to clean it, re-dress it and give you oral antibiotics. It should be fine. You carried her out of the canyon? No more heavy lifting," she scolds.

Later, she enters to tell me, "You're all patched up. Nothing a few more good meals and a good rest won't fix." She glances at the tray of empty dishes by my bedside. The person who delivered the food told me the meat was bovine. Some was cooked, some raw, all of it delicious, although I would have eaten it even if it 'tasted like ass' as Lumina would say.

The corners of my mouth tip slightly as I remember Lumina describing the *minten* that way. If she was awake now and had a working translator I would tease her about it. My guts squeeze in worry as I pray she wakes up.

"I'd like your permission to put you into a medically-induced coma just until tomorrow. I just read several research papers indicating the best way to recover from torpor and starvation is to put you out, hydrate you, and let you rest. What do you say?"

She's asking me to trust her? To put me into a coma?

"What about Lumina?"

"She's also out of it because of her concussion. Don't worry; she's going to be fine. How about this? I promise to wake you if she comes out of it. That way, you won't miss anything. Fair enough? You'll be much stronger and healthier by tomorrow."

I roll it around in my head for a minute, thinking of every eventuality, but I think if the doctor meant to harm me she would have done so already.

"Okay."

She injects me with something, and I fall asleep within seconds.

When I awaken the next day, I feel better than I have since I came to Earth. Strong. The doctor is standing in the doorway.

"These nice peacekeepers are going to get you to the Newcomer center," she says as five females dressed in combat uniforms file around her to enter my room. Their postures are on alert. They're all armed and seem to be taking their jobs very seriously.

"Have I been charged with a crime?" I sit up straighter, ready to jump out of bed and engage them in hand-to-hand combat if necessary. These females might be at the ready, but so am I. I've been fed, I'm warm, and they're not going to take me without a fight.

"No, Sir," the one in the lead says. She's all business, no smile on her face. "It has come to our attention that you're an unattended male. We've attempted to match your retinal scan with all legal newcomers, but find that you're off the books. Did you come here legally or were you brought against your will?"

I don't know enough about this planet. If I did, I'd be able to lie. As it is, I have to admit the truth. They clearly know I'm illegal if they cross-referenced their databases.

"Against my will."

"I regret any trouble this may have caused, Sir. Let me assure you that whoever did this has done so against planetary law. We're going to bring you to a Newcomer facility, give you a safe place to recuperate, and introduce you to Earth society."

I'm relieved to hear from these officials that stealing Draals is illegal here. Lumina wasn't lying, and perhaps the females of this planet aren't all as despicable as I thought.

"You'll be sent back to Draal at our expense when the next trans-port is ready to leave. In the meantime, you'll be treated as a valued guest and offered all the comforts we can provide. Should you wish to stay on this planet, we will welcome you and help you find a suitable mate—unless you fail our psychological tests. I've been told your body will mend fine and you have already met our physical requirements."

"I want to stay with Lumina." They're welcoming me? Offering all the comforts they can provide? This almost sounds too easy.

"I'm afraid that's not an option, Sir."

She offered and then rescinded? My brow lowers as I realize I don't like this female.

"Of course it's an option. You promised all the comforts, right? I've spent the last week with Lumina. She provides me comfort. No need to trouble yourself to take me to a facility."

"That's not the way it works, Sir."

"All the comforts," I prompt, my voice harsher. "I was brought to this planet illegally. You owe me this."

"First, we need to complete your psychological testing. Then your compatibility tests. Then, if you want a mate, you can choose from a list that your facility has properly vetted and will provide to you. All of that will be done at the closest Newcomer facility."

I sit straight up in bed, my eyes darting to all four corners of the room, wondering how I can manage an escape around the five females at the door—six if you count the doctor. I consider using my chameleon abilities. I could blend in with the bed or walls, but I still have body mass and couldn't sneak through the wall of flesh they present at the doorway.

"Where's Lumina? Is she okay? Is this a trick to keep me from finding out she's . . .?" I stare at the doctor, wordlessly challenging her to answer.

"Lumina is fine," the doctor reassures me. "She has a concussion and is still unconscious. We're attending to her and she'll recover fully."

"She can't be your mate, Sir," the military female continues. "She would have to go through all the proper channels to then be placed in line for a chance at obtaining a mate. We have many women who are eager to meet you, who have jumped through all the hoops and haven't pressed to the front of the line—"

"You can't do this!"

"Yes, Sir. We can and we will."

"I'm a captain in the Draalian army. What is your rank? I demand to speak to your superior."

"I'm a captain as well, Sir. I'm the ranking officer here. I'm following protocol."

"Your protocol is wrong!" I thunder. I look at the doctor. "Please. I need to see Lumina."

"Let me speak to the captain," is her answer. Am I reading her wrong? The warm look in her eyes shows compassion.

They go into the hallway and a few minutes later they return to the room.

"We'll allow you to see your companion if you follow our rules," the captain says. "Since you've indicated your reluctance to come with us, we'll only allow you to see her if you let us cuff your hands behind your back and agree to accompany us to our van afterward—without argument." Her chin is firm, her mouth forms a hard line, and she spears me with a challenging gaze.

I have no intention of getting into their van without argument, but I stand and put my hands behind my back. After I see Lumina and ensure she's safe, I'll make my escape.

"Here are some scrubs, Zoriss," the doctor says as she hands me a pale blue set of pants and shirt. "The waistband has a tie, but I imagine the legs will be far too short."

It's the first time I've worn anything resembling pants in days, so I don't complain. I think of all the time I was naked in the cave, and all the affectionate pleasure I could have shared with Lumina if I hadn't been so stupid. A pang of remorse forms a lump in my throat.

"Hands behind your back," the captain prompts after I'm dressed. I don't believe she's taking joy from this, although by the scent in the room, they all took joy from my display of naked skin as I dressed.

They secure me with a laser binding that's surprisingly strong. I'm not sure how I'll get out of this.

Two females flank me, with two in back and one in front. They're all well-armed, weapons drawn.

I don't know how to disarm them with my wrists tied tightly behind my back.

"We've set the weapons on stun, Sir. Believe me," the captain says, "I do not want to use them on you. We are very sorry you were brought here against your will and we'd like to make it up to you."

I consider telling her she can make it up to me by allowing me to stay with Lumina, but we've already exhausted that avenue.

I'm led into a room where my Lumina is hooked up to machines. How did I fail to notice how totally fucking beautiful she is? She's so pale, though.

I squat next to her, nestle my nose against her throat, and breathe in her essence.

"Here," one of them says as she pushes a chair under my ass so I can sit comfortably.

"Lumina," I whisper into her ear, "get a translator so when I return for you you can hear my words when I tell you how much I care about you and how sincerely I apologize. I'd stay if I could, but they're forcing me away at gunpoint. I'll come back for you."

"Sorry, Sir. We have to go."

"Doctor." I pierce her with my gaze. "Tell her how much I care about her. I fucked up and didn't tell her. Tell her I'm coming back for her."

"I will, Draalian."

"Tell her," I yell over my shoulder as they drag me from the room.

6

Lumina

Holy shit, my head is killing me. And my left arm. I try to open my eyes, but the light is so damn bright.

It takes me a moment to acclimate myself, but soon everything comes blasting back, starting with the crash, and immediately switching to thoughts of the Draalian. The handsome Draalian who was the male of my dreams. The ecstasy of our physical connection, the agony of his rejection.

Then a smile lights my face as I remember that moment as we were climbing up the canyon when everything changed. Dear God, the look in his eyes was so full of appreciation and apology.

"Zoriss?"

I force my eyes open to look for him. What I see is a sterile hospital room, well, two of them. I have double vision.

"Zoriss?"

A nurse comes running in. "May I help you?"

"Where's Zoriss?"

"The Draalian? He's gone."

My chest physically hurts. I understand the term "heartache" for the first time in my life.

"He . . . left?" Please God, tell me he left, and he's not dead.

She relays information from the chart and tells me how he convinced a stranger to bring us in, then how we were both medically treated.

"You have a concussion, I'm afraid."

That would explain the light sensitivity and double vision. She tells me they got him into a heated bed, fed him, and the doctor made certain the gash on his leg was properly treated.

"She made it a point of saying you did a great job considering you did it by firelight in a cave."

With an angry, uncooperative naked Draalian, I think, but don't say it out loud.

"You said he left?"

"Soldiers came to retrieve him. It sounds as if he was brought here to be sold on the black market. They're re-homing him and planning to give him the VIP treatment so he'll decide to stay." Her eyebrow raises, not once, but twice in an age-old expression of sexual interest.

"Tell me," her voice lowers to a conspiratorial whisper, "what was it like to be in close quarters with a hunk like that?"

Yeah, he's a hunk. Maybe that moment climbing up the crevasse was just that—a moment. Now that he realizes he can have any woman on the planet, maybe he'll be happy he has more choices than a female he hated for ninety-nine percent of our time together.

"He . . . just left? Just like that?"

"Oh, hell no. From what the grapevine says, they had to hand-cuff him and march him out of here at gunpoint. *Five* gunpoints to be exact. I wish I had been on shift to see that. They said he looked magnificent." She sighs dreamily. "At shift change, I was told he demanded to see you and wouldn't cooperate until they let him come in here."

"Really?"

"That's what I'm told. Blake was on duty. She said he came in, put his mouth to your ear and talked to you. She didn't catch a word of it, but she said it was the most romantic thing she'd ever witnessed."

"Really?"

Good. I wasn't just imagining our connection.

"So which re-homing facility did they take him to?"

"No idea."

"Can I see my chart?"

"That's against the rules, but you can speak with a doctor."

An hour later I've had not one but two breakfasts and am speaking with a doctor. I have a concussion, and she's suggesting I stay here another day, then convalesce at home on light duty.

"You'll probably have trouble concentrating for a while. Maybe dizziness and headaches. Post-concussive syndrome can last a few months to a year or longer if you don't treat it properly. You will need at least half an hour in a medtube every day for seven to ten days or until all the symptoms are gone."

"That male was certainly fond of you," she says. "Those peace-keepers had to drag him out of here to keep him away from you. He made me promise to tell you, and I quote, 'Tell her how much I care about her. I fucked up and didn't tell her. Tell her I'm coming back for her'." She spears me with a curious look. I guess she's waiting for my response.

"I'd like to go home now." I swing my legs over the side of the bed and fight the dizziness that's so intense it makes me nauseous.

"I wouldn't advise it."

"I'll be fine," I say, even though I have yet to place my feet on the floor.

She tries to dissuade me from leaving for a few more minutes, but eventually gives up.

After she leaves, I take my time getting dressed in my filthy, ragged clothes, then pay a security guard just getting off duty to take me back to my hover-car at the River of No Return Wilderness.

After she drives away, I sit in the car and breathe.

"You can do this, Lumina. You are going to find Zoriss. Just keep taking deep breaths and fight through it."

Which is exactly what I do.

I stop at the store on the way home to buy a top-of-the-line trans-lator. I walk up and down the aisles to grab enough food and drinks to last a week. I have a moment where I lose my balance and have to hold onto a sturdy shelving unit. Eventually the dizziness passes, and I carry on.

The first time I feel alive and truly believe I'll be able to find Zoriss is in my shower. I have to wash my hair four times before it's clean of pebbles, dirt, and grass. There are scrapes and abrasions all over my body, but I assume they've been sprayed with antibiotics and decide not to worry about them.

I lie down in my in-home medtube, glad it has taken care of all my medical needs up until now. I'd be happy to never have to darken the doors of a hospital again. It takes less than ten minutes for the AI bot to remove my old translator and insert the new one.

Not wanting to leave anything to chance, I turn on my computer to Draalian speech and nod my head when it translates perfectly.

I research where the nearest Newcomer facilities are. The closest one by far is near Beautiful View, a large city five hours from here. I take a chance this is where Zoriss will be, grab a few changes of clothes, and start my journey.

Zoriss

"Who is the supreme official of this planet?" I ask as we make our way to the facility. They were kind enough to untie my wrists from behind my back and retie them in front of me. All of this was accomplished with several lasers pointed at me. There was no way for me to make an escape.

Now we're driving through valleys nestled between mountains. I've seen few people, just grass, trees, and bovines.

"Planet President Farraday."

"I'd like to speak with her." I spear the captain in the front passenger seat with my most sincere look.

She has the audacity to stifle a smile. "I'm afraid that's not possible."

"You promised you would provide all the comforts. It would comfort me to speak with her to plead my case."

She takes a long breath as she appears deep in thought. "I have no more access to President Faraday than I could flap my arms and fly to the moon. That's way above my paygrade, Sir. What I can do, though, is have the Directrix of the facility speak with you as soon as you're settled into your dormitory. Would that be acceptable?"

"Does she have the authority to allow me to see Lumina?"

"I don't know."

Her eyes slide up and to the right. In my experience that indicates she's telling a lie, although I don't know if it's the same for humans as Draalians. The look on her face, though, reveals how uncomfortable she is.

"You're lying," I say quietly, but loud enough for her to hear. She doesn't deny it.

I close my eyes and pretend to sleep. I must be doing a good job of it because after a while the females begin to whisper.

"Whoever gets this one will be lucky."

"Shh. That's disrespectful. But . . . yeah."

"He certainly seems to want the woman in the hospital bed."

"Too bad for him that's not going to happen. The captain ran a search; she's not even on a list. He'll be scooped up by some lucky girl long before she has time to apply . . . and that assumes she even has the money."

"These reptilians were on the bottom of my list until a couple of hours ago. After seeing this one, they've moved to the top."

"When he was whispering in her ear? That was the single most romantic thing I've ever seen."

"Dreamy."

"I'm a sentient being, you know," I hiss as I open my eyes. "I have feelings, emotions. All females are not interchangeable. I've picked one already. Certainly exceptions can be made in cases like this."

They all have the decency to look embarrassed and contrite.

"I beg your pardon, Sir," the one sitting next to me says sincerely. "We shouldn't have spoken that way about you. None of us can help you, though. If we broke the rules about how females can obtain males, all hell would break loose across the planet. There are so many females and so few males. Everyone has to at least believe the rules are fair."

"And what about me? Is it fair to me that I'm to be torn from my female?"

She shakes her head, her lips clamped closed

Several hours later, I notice more traffic, then more buildings, and soon we arrive at the facility. It's a walled compound topped with spiked wire. I'm not sure whether it's to keep the valuable males protected or to keep them from escaping.

The barbed-wire gates close as soon as our vehicle's rear bumper clears the entrance. It appears there's a welcoming committee. Three Earth females are standing in front of the impressive facility, alongside them are two Draalian males. Something about seeing males from my homeworld comforts me.

"Mr. Krine?" one of the females says as she steps forward and nods.

"*Captain* Krine," I correct.

"My apologies, Captain. I'm Dylan Winters, Directrix here. This is Aidan Cane, your house manager, and Pat Cooper, her assistant. We thought you might want to meet a few other Draals. This is Pfall and Laang. They've been here awhile and will help get you acclimated.

"I can't tell you how sorry I am that you were brought here against your will. But I will tell you I personally will do everything in my power to make your stay here as pleasant as possible. Of course, it must be obvious we'd love for you to decide to stay on Earth."

Stay on Earth. This is the first time I've really considered the magnitude of this choice. All I've thought of since they told me they were moving me to this facility was that I wanted to be with Lumina.

Being with Lumina, though, means staying on Earth. Staying on Earth means never seeing my beloved clutchmate Zorn again. It means giving up my career in the military that I've served for close to half my life. My mother died several years back. I haven't had leave to return to Draal to visit her grave. Could I give all that up for a female I've never had a conversation with?

It's premature to make that decision. It is not too early to ask to see Lumina.

"I was pulled from a crashed escape capsule and nursed back to health by a female I'm now fond of. I'd like to be reunited with her."

"No one told me. You'd like to be mated to her? Which agency is she signed up with? Perhaps I could pull some strings and get her assigned to this one." She seems excited to help. Maybe this will be easier than I thought.

"I don't believe she had saved up for the fee yet."

"Oh." Her face caves in on itself. The brightness in her eyes fades. This isn't good news. "No one can jump the line, Captain Krine." She shakes her head, her face grimacing. "I can't make that happen."

My eyes slide to Pfall and Laang. If the females didn't have translators, I'd suggest we overpower them right here, right now. Even though the males don't look like they've been in the military, the three of us could probably take the eight females standing here, even though five of them are armed.

I don't make a secret of the fact that I'm assessing the facility boundaries and armaments. For all I know they're going to lock me in a cell. If I ever get a chance to make it out of the building and back onto the grounds, I'll need a strategy for escape. The barbed wire is canted out to prevent break-ins, not break-outs. Perhaps they were telling the truth when they said most males are here by choice.

"Let me show you to your room."

The room is spacious and furnished with clothes and toiletries. As mentioned, there's a basking rock under the window. This isn't what I pictured at all—it's nice. But I have no desire to stay. I want to find Lumina.

I admit, I'm excited to pull on a pair of pants that fit. Although it's a relief to speak with fellow Draals, they don't seem to understand my plight.

"The females are plentiful. And eager," Pfall says. "You'll find another. In fact, there's a mixer tonight. Eligible females come to meet us. They dress in their finest and are on their best behavior. It's shocking to go from having rarely seen a female my age to being desired by many." Pfall looks proud of himself.

"I've found several I could be happily mated to. I'm just having too much fun at these mixers to settle down," Laang says with a chuckle.

After they leave, I open the door to make certain it's not locked, then scout the hallways. There are cameras at every intersection and I don't know who is watching the feed.

At the hospital, I sat under the warming blanket for hours and fed really well. Using my camouflaging ability they won't see me on the camera. I think I'll be able to get to the wall and climb over it before anyone knows I'm gone. Then what will I do? Perhaps I need to get access to a computer and investigate what rights, if any, I have on this planet. Can they just round me up and incarcerate me?

Whatever the penalty, I need to find my way back to Lumina.

For the first time since I woke up on Earth, I'm in a room by myself. I sit on the upholstered blue rocker in the corner, close my eyes, and allow myself to relax. After a few moments of this, I'll be able to parse through my options and decide what to do.

Zorn! I feel my brother. My eyes pop open to look around as if he could possibly be in the room with me. He feels so close!

We were separated before, on Pythian. At one point we were almost on opposite sides of the planet. When I searched for him, his mental signature was almost non-existent. It proved that physical distance weakens the signal. I don't believe I could be receiving his signal from Draal.

Could he be on Earth? He has to be. He feels close. I try to determine his emotions. I search for anger, pain, fear . . . I don't feel it. Am I feeling my brother's . . . lust?

I replay the last events I remember before I woke up on the pirate vessel. Zorn and I had just emerged from our transport after five years off-planet. We were headed for some well-deserved rest and entertainment.

In the past, when we were on leave to Draal, our first stop was always home. We went to see our mother, who cooked our favorite dishes and lavished us with her love. We were both sad that on this furlough, the only place we'd see our mother would be at her grave. We lost her two years ago and went through the Draalian mourning period while away with our military. It didn't make our loss any less bitter.

As soon as we left our transport, we decided to head to a bar near the base and drink a pitcher of local brew. Now that I replay that evening in my head, I know the exact moment our *malenka* was drugged. A heavyset drunken Draal in an old uniform stumbled against our table, set it to right, apologized, and moved away.

Motherfucker! His voice was the voice of the pirate captain, the one who told us human females wanted our cocks and our sperm.

It never occurred to me until just this minute that Zorn was also on that transport ship. But of course he was. We were both drugged. My stomach heaves as I think he might have been lying in the stasis pod next to me on that ship and I never knew it.

Is he here? Was he brought to this Newcomer facility?

I use the comm they supplied me and call the female on duty. "Is there a Draalian here by the name of Krine other than myself? Zorn Krine?" my tone is urgent.

After a moment, she replies, "No, Sir."

After days of feeling dead space where our connection always was, to now feel him so close soothes my spirit.

"Might there be a Draalian here who has amnesia?" That would explain things.

"No, Sir. You're the only Krine here, and no amnestic Draalians."

"Thank you," I answer tersely, then terminate the comm.

It takes me only a moment to decide I want to find Lumina before I search for Zorn. I'm going to find them both, then make decisions from there. These ridiculous Earth rules that put protocol before the heart surprise me. You'd think Earthers would care less about a female's place in line than who she loved.

Love? Could Lumina love me? Why would she? I acted despicably. But I recall the look in her eyes when we stopped halfway up the steep ravine. She may not love me, but she cares for me.

And me? What are my feelings for her? It's too soon for love—for both of us. But all of that can be sorted out after I find her.

Lumina

I let the feeling of urgency propel me for hours, but I finally admit defeat. The needs of my body have conquered my emotional desire to drive nonstop to find Zoriss. I've pulled off the side of the road and am cradling my head in my palms. The headache is so fierce I take more painkillers than I should, then wait for them to kick in.

I shouldn't be driving—I'm seeing double—but as soon as I can bear it, I get back on the road. My nav says I'll be at the facility around nine tonight. I hope he's there. I know better than to call, though, they treat these guys like they're a state secret. Women are desperate for them. I guess that's why he's on Earth in the first place. He was abducted for God's sake.

As soon as my headache is down to a dull roar, I continue making my way to Beautiful View.

My mom always called me headstrong. I have to confess, I never admitted she was right until now. I shouldn't be driving and I know it. I should be at home in my medtube letting it calm the synapses in my head. I'd still have a concussion, but it would speed my recovery.

Instead, I'm racing down the highway toward the facility in Beautiful View praying that's where I'll find Zoriss. I have no idea how I'll get in to see him, though. The imbalance between women who want mates and the males who are here is shocking. When the first batch showed up, there were riots outside the facilities.

That's when all the facilities that were still under construction were built with reinforced concrete, and the existing ones were all retrofitted with barbed-wire fences around the exterior.

I guess mom was right when she called me impulsive as well as headstrong. I'm hurtling along this dark highway with no guarantee my Draalian will even be there, and even less chance that I'll be admitted.

I'm maybe an hour away when I see a disabled hover at the side of the road, a woman about my age standing nearby, looking bedraggled. For a split second, I actually consider pressing forward and waiting for another motorist to stop to help her. But we're literally in the middle of nowhere. I haven't seen another vehicle for twenty minutes, and frankly, I'm not a heartless bitch.

I slow my vehicle and turn around.

"Anything I can do?" I ask after I step out and approach her.

"I called for help. They won't be here for half an hour or more. I'll be fine." Her voice sounds upbeat, but the look on her face tells me she would welcome my company while she waits alone in the dark.

She's a pretty blond, with curly hair and a perky smile now that I've invited her into my veterinary van.

"I'm Taylor," she says around a bite of one of the nutrition bars I brought with me. "We look a lot alike."

"Lumina," I say as I inspect her more closely. Her hair is a few shades lighter than mine, but we both have heads full of natural curls. We have the same heart-shaped face and blue eyes.

"From a distance, yeah. What are you doing out in the middle of nowhere dressed like that?"

She's in a feminine pink dress that goes great with her coloring. It's not exactly what you'd expect to see on a rarely traveled road at eight in the evening.

"A mixer at the Newcomer facility."

I would expect to see a wide smile across her face, but she doesn't seem excited.

"You should act like you won the lottery. Why don't I see that on your face?" If it had been me a week ago on my way to a mixer, I wouldn't have needed a hover, I would have flown there on my own power.

"I've been to three of them already. It's a long drive there and back and so far, no one has sparked my interest. Well, and I haven't been any of their first choices either. Rejection isn't any fun."

"I'm shocked. You're so pretty. I can't imagine any male passing you up."

She laughs, "Of course you think I'm pretty, we could be sisters."

As she munches on her second bar she asks, "What are you doing out here in your sexy veterinarian van?" She smiles as she lifts one eyebrow in question.

"I'd tell you, but I'd have to kill you," I laugh as I hedge.

"Very funny. With a dodge like that, now I'm dying to know."

"Do you work in law enforcement?" I ask, knowing I sound like someone in one of the police procedurals I like to watch.

"No." She drags her answer into several syllables, her interest obviously piqued.

I decide to tell her everything. It's been a wild ride emotionally and physically and I haven't even told my best friend or my mom. It will be nice to unload to someone.

Ten minutes later, after word-vomiting out all my pain and anxiety to Taylor, I wipe my eyes and take a deep breath.

"This is so freaking romantic you've got me squirming in my seat. Listen, I've got it all worked out, but we have to work fast—the mech I called should be here soon. You're going to attend the mixer as me. I'll give you the invitation. I'll even let you wear my dress. I think it will fit. You can't go in the t-shirt and jeans you're wearing."

I imagine the torn, grass-stained clothes I was wearing earlier would have mortified her.

"I think you might be correct. In the right light we could pass for sisters, but don't they ask for identification?"

She heaves a sigh, then uses a conspiratorial tone to tell me, "I grew up the daughter of a rancher who was the daughter of a rancher. We live out in the middle of nowhere. Mostly it's a good life—fresh air, plenty to do—but it gets boring.

"In secondary school, I made my way to the part of Beautiful View nobody talks about. I procured a black market identity bracelet. It got me into some . . . interesting parties and allowed me to get alcohol and drugs. I'm a different person than I was then, but I never destroyed the bracelet. It even has almost a thousand credits on it, as I recall."

I'm not surprised to hear this. Almost everyone has gotten a false ID at some point in their teens.

"Strip," she says as she pulls off her dress. "As soon as I'm in your clothes I'll run to my car and get the ident bracelet."

"Don't you want to go to the mixer?"

"After the last three rejections, I wasn't looking forward to it. It won't hurt my place in line for a mate, I'll just go to the next one. Besides, it's so exciting to be able to help you break your Draalian out of there."

Break him out? My mind never got past the idea of breaking myself in. But, yeah, I think I'm going to break him out of there. And then what? We'll be like Bonnie and Clyde, hiding out for the rest of our lives? *One step at a time, Lumina.*

Twenty minutes later, the mech is working on Taylor's hover and I'm wearing a delicate pink dress that fits like a glove. Although it wouldn't have a week ago, I lost weight in that cave. I have her credit bracelet on my wrist and the invitation in my hand.

"Do you really think your plan for getting him out of there is going to work?" I ask.

"Unless they've changed their protocols? Yes."

"Taylor, I don't know how to thank you."

"Taylor Vale from Antiqua. Look me up. I want an invite to your mating ceremony."

Mating ceremony? Taylor's way ahead of me. First, she reminds me I'm going to have to break him out. Now she's got us mated already.

"You've got my head spinning," I tell her, reeling from the idea of mating a male I've never actually had a conversation with.

"Lumina, the way you looked when you talked about him . . . well, when you talked about the good parts of him, I wouldn't have to be a fortune teller to believe there's going to be a mating in your future."

After a heartfelt hug, I hover off. An hour later, I pull up to the facility. It looks like a maximum-security prison from vids about the olden days. There's barbed wire surrounding the entire facility. Shit. How is this going to work?

Zoriss

I don't know why I allowed Laang and Pfall to talk me into coming to the mixer. I guess I wanted to experience being in a room full of females at least once in my life. Having only been around my mother, my two aunts, and otherwise all males, it's interesting to feel an actual difference in the energy in the room.

They've tried to make it festive; it's draped with ribbons and bows and there is food everywhere. But it's not the decorations that are the most prominent feature of the room, it's the smell of female arousal that assaults the nose from every corner.

Then there are the females themselves. There are redhairs and brownhairs and goldenhairs. There are curlyhairs and straighthairs and shorthairs and longhairs. There are tall ones and short ones. Some females are modestly dressed, some have breasts falling out of their tops. They're getting the most attention, although I'm not sure how many of those will get serious mating proposals.

Now that I'm used to human features, I don't find these females bland or unattractive as I initially did with Lumina. Not one of them, however, is nearly as beautiful as my Lumina.

My Lumina. I worry about how she's doing. The female in charge of outgoing comms said she was given strict orders not to allow me to contact her. It doesn't bother me too badly. As soon as everyone goes to sleep tonight, I'll sneak out of the barracks, climb the wall, and head north to find her.

At one point in her anxious babblings, she mentioned her home city. I'll make my way there and find her.

A few of the women have asked me to dance. I guess I should take it as a compliment when a human approaches me, eyes luminous and full of interest, and hands me the stiff slip of paper with her comms information and her first name on it in English and all three alien languages of the males on the planet. It is the way the facility conducts the dance so that couples can meet and begin the process they call 'dating'.

Although I wonder what it would feel like to dance with a female, I have no desire to do it with anyone but Lumina.

I'm holding my hands behind my back in the 'at ease' position we use in the military. I hadn't even noticed a female approach me until I feel one pass a stiff piece of paper into my palm. I turn to politely tell her no when I'm struck speechless.

This female looks exactly like my Lumina. She acts shy, just like the other females did when they approached me. Perhaps human genetics differ from Draalians'. Could two females look exactly alike?

"Care to dance, Draalian?"

And could they sound exactly alike? My heart expands in my chest. This isn't Lumina's double. This beautiful female is Lumina.

"Lumina?" I ball my fists, accidentally crunching the slip of paper in my effort not to pull her into my arms and kiss her with the force of the Miriain meteor shower.

"Call me Taylor," Lumina's mouth tells me, but her eyes are roaming over me as if she wants to tear my clothes off and continue where we left off on the floor of the cave back in the canyon.

"Pleased to meet you, Taylor," I say as I drag her against me and move across the floor.

"I saw you from across the room and just knew you were the male I wanted to dance with all night long," she says.

Most of my brain believes this is the female I just spent the last week with, but part of me still wonders if she has a double. How did Lumina find me? And how did she sneak in? This place is guarded as well as the presidential palace back on Draal. And she understands what I'm saying. Did she get a new translator?

"Ever heard of a place called the River of No Return?" I ask, trying to be sly.

"Heard of it? I met the most *shamispah* Draalian on Earth there." Her eyes are twinkling.

I dance us to a dark corner in the back, trying to hide the smile on my face. This removes all doubt of who, exactly, is in my arms.

I know we're not invisible back here, but we're partially hidden, and we're not the only couple barely dancing as we hold each other in the shadows.

"In a moment, I'm going to ask you about your concussion and how you managed to not only find me, but sneak your way into this dance. But right now, Lumina. This. Just this."

I pull away, grip her shoulders, and drink in the sight of her. I allow my blue tongue to slip between my lips to smell her, barely stifling a hiss as I catch her scent. She's cleaner than I ever experienced her, and I smell her arousal as it floats to me on the humid room air.

She shivers.

"Cold?"

She doesn't answer, just shakes her head.

"Ah, as I remember, you like my tongue."

"Handsome, sexy, despicable male," she scolds, a close-lipped smile brightening her face. "Don't you know it's considered impolite to discuss such things in public?"

I pull her closer, one hand on the small of her back, the other on the delicate nape of her neck. "Is that right? I know so little of the social norms on Earth. So that I can follow the rules, would it be rude to mention that I haven't stopped thinking of you since we parted?"

"No. That would be fine."

"And to ask how you're feeling?"

"Also in good taste. I'm pretty good. Just a small headache and occasional double vision which is a bonus, by the way, when I'm looking at a certain handsome Draalian male."

I laugh. "So good to know. Very reassuring. Just to get this straight, would it be impolite to mention that if I concentrate for just a moment I can actually conjure your taste in my mouth."

Her pink lips pop open in surprise. She doesn't have to answer my question for me to know that my comment just shocked her. Her pink cheeks announce the fact.

"So I guess it would also be impolite to mention I miss the way you moan when you come apart underneath me?"

"Zoriss?" Is she asking me to stop, or wanting me to continue?

"And painting a word picture, telling you how beautiful you were in the firelight, sweating from exertion even though the air was frigid, your nipples pulled into hard points from wanting me? Would that break a social norm?"

She nods as if she's hypnotized, under a spell. *My* spell.

"Then I shouldn't mention that sheathing myself in your body was the single highest honor and privilege I've ever been afforded in my life."

Her hands slide up my back and stroke my nape. She presses my shoulders lower so she can whisper in my ear.

"I like understanding the words coming out of your mouth." She sneaks the tip of her tongue into my ear.

"I want to dance with you, Lumina. But before we do anything else I need to apologize."

"It's okay—"

"No. It's a big ugly thing between us. I don't want it there. There are things that must be said."

She nods, then looks at me as if she's afraid of what I'm going to say.

"Don't worry, sweet, only one of us is *shamispah*, and it isn't you." I pause a moment, drinking in the sight of her, so happy we're warm and clothed and together. Most of all, I'm thrilled to see the affectionate gaze in her blue eyes.

"I was drugged and thrown onto a transport. They locked me in a stasis pod. I've been in them a dozen times before, but this time the drug that puts you to sleep didn't work properly. It paralyzed me but left me wide awake.

"I laid like that for three of your months unable to move, unable to open my eyes or stretch or scratch an itch. The only thing I had for company was my own thoughts. Well, my own thoughts and the endless loop of information about Earth they relentlessly piped into the pod.

"When they were about to open the stasis pods, they told us the reason we were brought here was for our cocks and our sperm. We were auctioned and bought before we even landed. Because I was never knocked unconscious, when they finally allowed us to move, I was fast enough to make a run for an escape capsule. As you know, I had a hard landing.

"I lost my memory at first, and my attraction to you was immediate and powerful. That first night, that was the true Zoriss, the one who cares about you." I pull her hand to rest on my cheek, then turn my head to kiss her palm.

"You said something that unlocked my memories. They bombarded me, and my outrage at my abduction was so hot it overrode everything else. I was furious, and you were the only person I could take it out on.

"The male you met had marinated in agony and anger for three months with one thought and only one thought pulsing through his brain—revenge. Well, two thoughts. The second was hatred. Hatred toward all evil Earth females who would steal a male from his life in order to force him to Earth for their own desires."

She presses her lips to the scales exposed above my collar. "I'm sorry."

"Don't be. You didn't earn it. I've played it over and over in my head, wondering if your translator had worked if things would have been different. If the whole misunderstanding could have been cleared up in the first hour. But we'll never know.

"What I do know . . ." I grip her shoulders and pull her away from me so she can look into my eyes. "What I do know is that I made the biggest mistake of my life. You're kind and loving and generous. You saved my life, Lumina. I would have bled out in that escape capsule without your help."

This beautiful female is perfect. Instead of hating me, she's looking at me like I'm the best male in the room. No, the best male on Earth. I don't warrant this level of affection and acceptance.

"And I would have slipped into torpor in the cave if you hadn't generously shared your warmth with me despite the way I had treated you. And the intimacy? Lumina, that was so much more than a male like me could hope for. You're a good female and I'm lucky to have met you."

She presses tightly to me, her chest squeezed to mine. I feel her swiftly beating heart.

"Tell me you're sorry one more time," she says, her gaze spearing mine.

"I'm truly sorry. Repentant. I'd do anyth—"

"Thanks for the apology and the explanation. Now I understand. It's over. I don't want to hear it again. I want to go forward, not back."

My chest clenches in gratitude. I don't deserve this female.

I drop a kiss on her mouth. It's a sweet, superficial kiss. If I allow myself to do anything more intimate, I fear I won't be able to control myself.

We continue to shuffle, pretending to dance while we bask in each other's embrace.

"Zoriss," Pfall says from a foot away. "Laang and I decided one of us should come over and tell you the music has ended."

I tip my head to listen. Sure enough, it's quiet. We're the only couple still locked in a clinch as everyone else heads to the banquet table.

"I figured if I didn't interrupt, you might mount the female right here on the dancefloor."

I tip my head as I contemplate. Although he thinks he just told a joke, in my mind it's still an option.

"I knew your insistence that you didn't want to dance with a female wouldn't last long. Whoever you were pining over will fade from your mind in a few days."

"You're a lucky female," he says to Lumina. "He was a captain in the Draalian army."

"Really? How do I know you're both not just lying to impress me?"

"If you get farther in the process you'll see the metal armcuff around his bicep. If it has a ruby, it signifies he's a captain." He turns and calls over his shoulder, "Have fun."

"Good to know," she calls to his retreating back.

A smile lights her face. I imagine we're both thinking of her hand on it in the cave's firelight. "And here I thought it was there just to look sexy, Captain."

"You think it's sexy?"

"I think *everything* about you is sexy."

"I love that you're incapable of lying." Our gazes lock together and we can't hide our aroused smiles. "Tell me how you're going to get me out of here. No. First, tell me how you got in here in the first place."

Lumina

I tell him about Taylor. As I do, it dawns on me how generous she was to do this for me. If I was *shamispah* I would just use her ticket and agree to mate him under her name. She'd be out of luck and I'd be hitched.

But of course, I'm not that female.

"Taylor's been to three of these events before. She said the place is heavily defended against people breaking in, but not at all protective of people leaving.

"All the males are here by choice. The last thing they would want to do is leave. The females who were lucky enough to make their way inside wouldn't do anything to jeopardize their good standing. They even allow the males to walk the females to their hovers. You're just going to hop inside, slip into the back, and wait until we're out on the road to come sit in the front with me."

"Then what?"

"Yeah . . . after that I have no idea. We're going to be on the run. Honestly, the farthest I got was to wonder if we'd wind up living in that cave at the bottom of the canyon for the rest of our lives."

"That might have its appeal." He cocks his browridge and gives me a sweltering look.

I grimace, though, remembering the hard stone floor, the freezing cold, and the nutrition bars. "Not really."

"There are so many things I didn't have the opportunity to tell you, Lumina. I have a brother."

Very interesting, although I'm not sure why he needed to divulge that right this very moment.

"He's my clutchmate. On my planet, clutchmates all have a psychic bond. Some are stronger than others. Ours was very powerful. I'm convinced he's on Earth. I feel him. I think he's nearby. We don't exactly talk through our link. It's more like we . . . feel each other. I need to reunite with him. The connection between us is strong enough I believe we can find him."

"That would be wonderful for both of you. But I'm not certain how that will help *us*."

"It sounds as if staying on Earth together won't be an option. The military females told me you not only have to pay all the fees, you have to get in line. They said I'd be mated or sent back to Draal before that could happen. I propose we find Zorn, then the three of us can go back to Draal together.

"I would quit the military and get a job. You might be able to become a vet, or a doctor since you're well-versed in reptiles. We could have a life there. I would do everything in my power to make you happy, Lumina. I would be honored if you would even consider it."

He's looking at me so sincerely, he has to see the blood drain from my face. I feel my extremities go numb. At first, I'm shocked to hear his proposal. Two days ago, he hated me and I wasn't too fond of him—at least outwardly. But I can't kid myself. I'd love to be mated to him.

Then I consider what he just proposed. He wants me to leave Earth with him. I never considered things would get this far.

My palm is splayed on his chest. I feel his heart beating under his scales. Isn't this what I wanted? To meet a Draalian? To fall in love? To have him looking at me the exact way Zoriss is looking at me right this minute?

"We'll stay on the run until we find your brother. Then we'll go home for me to say goodbye to my mother. Then we'll take the transport to Draal." I can't believe I said that. My heart is breaking.

Now I can better imagine how hard this was for Zoriss. For him to leave his planet and everything he holds dear when it wasn't even his choice. No wonder he was so full of rage when his memories returned.

"You don't have to make the decision right this minute. I'm happy you're even considering it, Lumina. I could never find my way to Zorn without you. I don't know your customs, your money, or even how to drive a human hover. I'm grateful you're willing to help.

"After we find Zorn, maybe you'll find me *shamispah* again. Or you'll decide you don't want to leave everything you know, everyone you love. I won't hold you to your offer. But I would appreciate it if you stayed with me until I find my brother."

"You're a good male, Zoriss. I'd be happy to help."

We dance for another hour or more. At one point he slips to his room and returns bulkier.

"Gain some weight?" I ask.

"I was cold every second in that cave. I'm taking all the clothes they loaned me. Layers!"

"Be prepared. A good motto."

Once I'm dancing in his arms again, you'd never know both of us were in the hospital mere hours ago, or that we could both use some sleep. What you'd know if you bothered to look at us, is that whatever happened in the cave in the canyon is almost forgotten.

Whatever hurt feelings and misunderstandings occurred are no longer on the top of our minds. What is in our thoughts is the connection we forged and the attraction we're experiencing right this moment.

A few women have drifted out in ones and twos, but now a large contingent is leaving. Several aliens are walking them to their hovers.

"Perfect timing, Zoriss. Want to walk me to my hover?"

"There's nothing I'd like more." He offers me his arm, I hang onto it, and off we go.

Although I feel like a bank robber, we raise no suspicions. We're just an Earth female and a Draalian male who met at a mixer and want to steal a kiss in the cool night air. As paranoid as I am, no one is watching or counting male heads. Zoriss slips into my van.

"Do you mind hiding in the back until we're well beyond the gates?"

"Okay," he slides into the cargo area as we'd discussed, and I get in line to wait for the gate to open.

I panic as I see two dormitory guards check every vehicle. They have their laser flashlights out and are opening doors and having everyone step out.

"Crap! Zoriss. They must have changed their protocol since Taylor was here! They're checking everyone!" My hands start vibrating in fear. We were so close to escaping. Now they're going to apprehend him, maybe confine him to his room. They'll not only confirm every terrible belief he ever had about humans, but they'll separate us and never give us a chance to be together.

"Don't worry," he says. Perhaps he doesn't understand how serious this is. Otherwise, how could he sound so confident?

I hear him rummaging in the back. It's a well-stocked vet van I use when I do rural house calls to doctor big animals. It's an open cargo area with cabinets along the walls. There's nowhere to hide.

"Zoriss! What can we do?" my voice sounds high and frantic.

I'm petrified and already mourning his loss. We've just found each other and worked out our misunderstandings. It's not fair. "I don't want to lose you!"

"Don't worry, Lumina. I'm a Draalian, remember?"

My brain is frozen. I have no idea what he's talking about.

I hear him come up front and feel something brush by me, but I see nothing.

"I've lost my mind, Zoriss. I think there's a ghost in here and I don't believe in ghosts."

"Calm down, Lumina. I'm right here."

His warm palm wraps around my forearm, but I don't see him.

"You've wanted a Draalian male for years. Have you forgotten we can camouflage?"

"Dear God," I say as I slap my palm on my chest and command my heartbeat to slow. "I totally forgot." I heave a huge sigh and glance to my right. He is absolutely invisible.

"That is amazing."

"Wait until I get you alone tonight, Lumina. I want to hear you say that in bed."

"Are you gloating? You are so *shamispah*."

"Perhaps you got the meaning wrong. It doesn't mean fabulous."

"I know that!"

"Or wonderful."

"You're actually joking with me when I just almost had a heart attack?"

"You think it means sexy, right?" Even though I can't see him I imagine his browridge lifting seductively.

"Despicable." I double down.

I count my breaths as the two guards inspect the van. I count four while breathing in and four breathing out. My heart is still racing out of control, but luckily, they don't have a clue. After less than a minute, they wave us through the gate.

We drive in silence for a while. When I glance over, sure enough, there's a very handsome and very naked Draalian on my right. And, just as I suspected he's gloating playfully.

"Don't be so impressed with yourself," I scold. "Just because I can't camouflage myself doesn't mean I don't have skills, too."

"I'm very aware of your skillset," his voice has that deep husk he only uses when he's talking about sex.

"Are you sure you'd never been with a woman before? You're pretty damn sure of yourself. Cocksure," I say as I giggle.

"Are you trying to hurt my feelings? Because actually you're giving my ego a boost." He grabs my hand and smiles at me.

"Which way?" I ask when the facility is no longer on any of my screens.

"Northwest."

"I'm tired, Zoriss. Mind if I find a place to stop once we're an hour or so from here?"

"I wouldn't mind finding a bed." He pauses for effect. "Sleep would be nice too."

"Sleep first, then the other? I really need to rest." I press my hand to my forehead as if that would make me feel better.

"Teach me to drive this. I've driven anti-grav vehicles in the army. I just can't read your language."

Fifteen minutes later, he competently hovers away. I watch him drive for a few minutes and as soon as I'm sure he's got the hang of it, I allow myself to drift off, hoping my headache will be gone when I awaken.

"Lumina!"

Zoris's voice pulls me from a deep sleep. I wake, frantic. Are we in trouble?

"Is that a sleeping facility?" he asks. The hover is going as slow as it possibly can while still staying in the air.

"Well, perhaps we should define sleeping facility."

The motel I see is a relic from the last century. We're out in the hinterlands. I didn't expect to find a fabulous hotel, but this barely qualifies as a motel. It definitely doesn't qualify as fabulous.

"Yeah. Pull over."

It's an antique that screams 'shabby' and couldn't have been anyone's idea of a dream getaway even in its heyday. On the other hand, anything softer than stone and warmer than frigid would be a step up from our cave.

"I'll do the talking," I say as we enter the small shacklike office.

The faint odor of mold assaults us as soon as we cross the threshold. The small reception area has two grungy orange chairs and poor illumination, possibly designed to keep patrons from noticing how seedy the place is.

Behind a wall, the top half of which is glass, is a blowsy woman whose dark black hair has two-inch white roots. Her face is pinched, and you'd have to be blind not to see her blatant disapproval of my traveling companion.

"We don't—"

I slam my palm down hard on the ancient counter that separates her from us.

"Before you insult an honored Draalian guest by refusing him service, let me introduce myself," I say in my haughtiest voice. "I am Lumina Malone, one of the board members of what used to be called Project Ark and is now part of the Repopulation Initiative. Our government has gone to great trouble and expense to get quality males like this to come to Earth. I would hate for you to be cited for hate speech or non-cooperation with this Newcomer. What were you about to say?" I lift my eyebrow, waiting.

"We have just one room and it's a king." She spears me with an angry look as if to say, "he can stay but you'll have to bunk together. I hope this mortifies you."

"It's our lucky day, honey," I toss over my shoulder, then fill out the form on her prehistoric computer pad. When I hand it back to her, she's not looking at me, she's looking over my shoulder at Zoriss. Her eyes are wide in . . . what, fright? disgust?

When I turn around, I see my Draalian captain standing tall in his black jeans and t-shirt. His facile blue tongue is sticking between his lips, its two halves twining and untwining over and over as he stares at her. It's a beautiful, impressive sight to a woman who's about to reap the benefits of its ability to perform gymnastics. It is probably disturbing as hell to someone who doesn't think aliens should be on this planet in the first place.

As I place my finger on the digital pad that will take my fingerprint to allow me into the room, I hear the word "wog," spoken in barely a whisper. Her expression challenges me to say something, although I know she'll just deny it. I curb my impulse.

Wog. How is it that idiots like her have the brains to come up with a myriad of creative, hateful names to call their supposed enemies? Wog for pollywog. Bitch.

"Want him printed?" she asks as if he was incapable of speech.

Do I? Do I want him close enough to her to hear the poison she's going to spew, albeit in a furious whisper?

You bet your ass I do. He's a captain in the Draalian army. Then I realize he was probably printed at the facility and the authorities would be here in minutes.

My feisty guy is no wimp, though. He makes a preemptive strike by innocently asking, "Do you by any chance have any crickets, Ma'am? I've discovered they're delicious."

We watch as the harridan's face crumples, nose wrinkling, throat convulsing as if she's about to vomit. Zoriss sees his enemy's weakness and strikes again, "No crickets? How about cockroaches? They'll do in a pinch."

"Room 117," she tosses over her shoulder as she lurches toward a back room.

"Well played, Captain, well played."

Luckily, our room is cleaner than the motel lobby. After checking for bedbugs, I pull off my clothes and fall into bed. My temples are throbbing, but not so badly that I don't enjoy the striptease Zoriss entertains me with.

After we fled the barracks, he put back on several layers. Once we got to our room, he started tearing off his clothes to join me. After he noticed my interest, though, he slowed down and camped it up. I'm now enjoying the removal of his third and final layer as he waggles his cute blue tush at me.

"When I wake up and my head isn't pounding, you're going to remind me what you taste like, Captain."

"Threat?"

"Promise."

He climbs in and places my head on his shoulder, then gazes at me, a soft look of appreciation on his face.

"It's . . ." He trails off as he cocks his head and stares at me.

"What?"

"Do you know how many miracles had to happen for us to be together like this?"

"How many?"

"Well, I'm not sure I want to call my abduction a miracle, but after that I had to escape a fiery crash, you had to rescue me, and you had to stop my artery from bleeding out."

"You had to carry me to safety after I tumbled down a steep ravine and broke myself," I chime in.

"And you had to meet a nice female named Taylor who got you into the facility. And now we're here with that wonderful human at the front desk. She is just what I pictured all Earth females to be."

"Luckily, she's in the minority," I tell him.

His eyes inspect the ceiling. "Think she's got cameras? Think she's watching?"

I snuggle closer and tell him. "When I wake up and my head quits hurting, let's give her a show."

Zoriss

Lumina fell asleep almost as soon as we turned out the lights. I stayed up longer, just looking at her by the illumination trickling in through the antique blinds. I was busy enumerating all the miracles that got us to this place. I didn't want to speak it out loud, but we're going to need several more miracles in order to stay together.

Zorn and I have been traipsing around the galaxy with the military. Since our mother died, we barely kept up with Draalian news. We get home so rarely it isn't part of our day-to-day concerns.

I only learned about the Earth mating exchange when I saw it on a vid at the bar where we were drugged and abducted. Although I invited Lumina to come back to Draal with me, I have no idea if it's even a possibility.

Shaking my head, I try to keep myself from falling down a deep mental hole, then pay attention to Lumina's warm skin on mine. She's practically burrowed into me, one leg thrown over my hips, an arm flung across my waist, and her lips on my pec as if she fell asleep mid-kiss.

For a male who has believed his whole life that he would never know romantic love, I have no doubts that is what my heart is feeling right now.

Tamping down my urge to kiss her awake, I let her sleep. It was obvious her head was hurting. I don't want to wake her up. I let myself fall asleep knowing I'll open my eyes to my Lumina when I awaken.

"I thought I'd never wake you," she giggles hours later when my eyes pop open from a deep sleep.

"Brazen female!" I accuse. My naked female is riding me. "How long have you been doing that?"

"Long enough that your belly is coated with my cream."

She looks quite proud of herself. Her hips don't miss a beat as she drags her slick folds across my scales.

"You're beautiful," I say as I hold the weight of her breasts in my palms.

"You used to talk during sex back in the cave. It was the only time your voice was sweet. I always wondered what you were saying."

"You're about to find out. It's not going to be pretty."

Her gaze whips to mine, her brows clenched in worry.

"You're going to know all the warm praises I didn't want you to understand."

"Warm praises?" She's smiling again, her blue gaze heated.

I pull her up my body, then press her torso toward me so I don't have to move to suck her nipple into my mouth. This feels new, being able to speak with her, but we were together in the cave long enough that her body learned to communicate with mine very well.

I suck until her nipple is plump and needy, then scrape the tip. Today I use the little fangs that protrude from my top jaw until she squeals a high note, then moans deep and low. She must have been riding me for a while. She usually doesn't make these noises until we've been at it a while.

"You started without me, Lumina? Naughty."

"*Shamissspah*," she nods, trying to smile, but too aroused to keep her mouth from popping open with a gasp of pleasure.

"Indeed." I move my attentions to her other breast, my fingers plucking the moist one my mouth just abandoned.

She wiggles, rearranging herself so her wet folds surround my primary, riding it.

"Promise me," she says, then pauses as she pants in delight, "we'll never wait this long again."

"Never," I lie, knowing I shouldn't make promises I can't deliver.

Lumina

This feels so good I don't want to prolong it. I want to impale myself on his secondary and find the bliss we perfected in that cave even when we hated each other—or tried to. But I want something different.

He has two cocks. I want to experience that.

I have to admit, my Draalian sexbot's primary went unused. I wasn't ready to try that. But I am with Zoriss.

135

He was planning on it. In the cave, he was preparing me. When I couldn't understand his words it was a bit daunting. As mean as he was during the day, though, when we shared the blankets at night, his voice was soft and seductive. And his hands were always gentle, even as his fingers explored the place that had never been breached.

Although he's always been able to understand me, it's a new thing for me to understand him, for us to have two-way communication. I'm fearful of his rejection although I have no reason to be.

"I want both tonight, Zoriss." I pierce him with a serious look. Although I'm certain he knows what I mean, I add, "both cocks."

"Are you sure you're ready?" He tilts his head to get a better look at me.

I nod.

He flips me onto my back in one smooth move and climbs between my thighs as he opens me wider. When he nips up my thigh, I moan and shiver as he draws his fangs along the sensitive flesh.

He licks at the seam where my thigh meets my torso, teasing me mercilessly, then stabs his tongue into me without warning.

"Zoriss!" My fingers bite into his muscular shoulders as my fingertips register the patterned scales.

We've been here before, in the cave. Once he's tasted me it's like a military attack that doesn't stop until he can declare victory. And victory only comes after I do—many times.

He lifts my legs, draping them over his shoulders to get a better angle, and groans deep and long and low as if he's eating his last meal. His little bump of a nose rubs my clit back and forth until I'm begging. It's only then that a thick finger slides into me as his talented tongue surrounds my clit.

My mind flashes me a picture of the way he furled and unfurled the two halves of his tongue to scandalize the woman who checked us in. The picture certainly doesn't offend me, though. It's hot as hell.

My release builds within me, gathering like the perfect storm. At first, I'm aware that my lips transform from overly sensitive to almost numb. My highly sensitized thighs are long forgotten. Even the delicious sensations in my breasts grow unimportant as my clit becomes the center of my universe. My clit and my core.

He works my body as if he has an owners' manual. No. As if he *wrote* the owners' manual. I howl when I come, unable to contain the burst of joy and pleasure as my whole world narrows to just the two of us and my physical bliss.

He bites and nips his way up the center of my body, past my rib cage, up the valley between my breasts, and bestows the sweetest kiss on my panting lips. He tastes like me. It's a testament to our intimacy.

"I never got to tell you how much I love your taste, how your scent is an aphrodisiac. There's so much I want to share with you, Lumina."

I kiss him hard.

"I want to share with you, too, Zoriss. Make love to me like it should be for you. Like a Draalian."

His palms slide down my sides.

"Your body should be worshipped," his voice is more growl than speech.

"No argument from me, Captain."

After swirling his finger in my cream, he swipes it on my tight pucker. In the cave, the first time he did it, I almost died of embarrassment. Soon after that, though, I almost died of need. It ramped me up and scandalized me in equal measures. After that, the embarrassed shyness disappeared, and I yearned for it.

One finger breaches me, evoking a throaty moan and a thrust of my hips.

I want to say his name, but all that escapes my lips is the last letter, "Sss."

He slides another finger inside, slowly, barely penetrating me, then slips it deeper as it joins the first.

"Okay?"

"Better than okay."

Leaning to kiss me, keeping my mouth busy with kisses and avoiding his sharp fangs, his fingers scissor open and closed. We never got this far in the cave. I understand the phrase 'hurts so good' now.

"We'll go slow," he breathes into my mouth. "Betharn wasn't built in a day."

"Neither was Rome. Let's try."

He grabs my hips and thrusts his primary into my core in one long, even, smooth move. It's the first time he's breached me with his primary. He's big. Bigger than my sexbot at home. The scales wake up every nerve ending inside me, or maybe it's all the Draalian bumps and ridges.

"I'm going to make you come again, sweet. One more time just for fun."

He's smiling, but instead of hiding his fangs like usual, he displays them prominently. Pointing out our differences instead of our similarities. It makes my heart skip a beat.

"Bite me with them," I demand before I even realize I had the thought.

"Absolutely. Another time, though," his voice is so rough it barely sounds like him.

He pounds into me. His angle is just right so his slick secondary slides along my little bundle of nerves, arousing me with every thrust.

Dipping his head, he growls, "Now," into my ear. And I come. On command.

When I reach it, this orgasm is so powerful, the muscles in my throat strain as I grunt with the effort.

"You're so beautiful," he croons into the shell of my ear even as his hips don't miss a beat while pistoning into me.

As I float down from my physical high, like a feather slowly drifting to earth, he lifts my thigh, reaches beneath it, and presses his primary against my back hole. It's slicked from having been in my core.

Then he stops, looking at me for approval.

"Go for it, Draalian."

He presses with sexy hip thrusts. I'm sensitized and needy. My barriers are down. I'm filled with the primal urge to have him inside me. For him to take me, to own me, everywhere.

He stops, just the head of his cock inside me as we wait for my body to accept him. My sphincter tries to push him out for a moment, but he stills, refusing to relinquish the ground he fought so hard to gain.

My body rejects the pain signals it's receiving and identifies them as pleasure instead.

"Shit," I say, not knowing how else to narrate the physical bliss I'm experiencing. He reads me completely wrong and almost retreats.

"Forward," I entreat, the word barely a breath. "Captain."

And the onslaught continues. We grunt in unison with every thrust. Every inch he gains is a sensual victory—until I'm full. Just to drive home the point, he presses once, twice more to make certain he can't penetrate me even one millimeter more.

His handsome face is thrown back, his Adam's apple prominently displayed, the muscles in his throat straining. He swallows with effort, his eyes closed as he appears to be swimming in bliss.

I feel full, taken, owned. So connected I know in my heart nothing can tear us asunder. Nothing.

"Two, Love?" he asks, his gaze inspecting my face, examining for reluctance. He's not going to find any.

After notching his secondary at my core, he glides in slowly, all the while whispering in my ear and telling me how good this feels, how tight I am.

Tight? Hell yes. Full. Taken. Both his cocks are in me. It's right and good and perfect. He's exactly where he should be. It's physical and mental and emotional. It washes away the crazy mixed messages of the cave and replaces them with the sublime connection we're experiencing now.

I can't wait another moment to race to the finish line.

"Fuck me," I demand.

It's like the starting gate opened at a horse race, where the horses transform from still to explosive movement from one heartbeat to the next.

Every muscle in his body moves with grace and power as he sheds all inhibitions and pounds into me. Every deep thrust is a statement of his need, his caring, his desire. For me, for us, for now, and for the future.

It's too much. Too overwhelming. Between the physical and emotional overload, I don't feel like an active participant. It's as if I'm watching a cataclysm, a tsunami, a wall of bliss a thousand feet high that's barreling at me a thousand miles an hour. When it hits, it's both a shock and a foregone conclusion.

I scream so loud it shocks me, yet I have no desire to tone it down or control it. Covering my mouth with his, he moans into me as he releases. I feel his powerful jets inside my ass, only now realizing I've never felt him ejaculate before. I remember it's only Draals' primaries that release.

Right this moment I want to keep riding the blissful wave of pleasure until the deluge of delight turns into a manageable flow.

At times I talk too much, like when I'm anxious or uneasy or even sometimes when I'm happy. But this minute I can't speak at all. There are so many consonants and vowels and words and sentences and paragraphs whirling in my head I don't know where to start. I want to praise him and vomit out my feelings to him. I want to talk about the future—both my dreams and my worries.

There's too much, so I clamp my teeth together, then, for good measure, I press my lips shut and just watch the whirlwind of thoughts circle in my head.

I can, however, let my body eloquently speak to the handsome man in my arms. Somehow, we're lying, our heads on the almost-flat pillows, and my palm is pressed against his muscular pec. I stroke him, letting my hands do the talking.

Dipping his head to kiss the top of my head, he makes a little hum in the back of his throat.

"I never dreamed, not for a second, not seriously, that I'd have that, Lumina. Let's add that to the list of miracles. Thank you."

He shouldn't have to thank me. It was a gift—freely offered. But the fact that he did, in that sincere tone of voice, makes me tear up in happiness.

"I *did* dare to dream it, Zoriss. But I never believed I'd have it. Thank *you*."

Zoriss

I wake to an empty bed. After a night cuddling next to the furnace of my warm-blooded female, I feel a new kind of chill —empty.

She's pacing. Even during our worst moments in the cave, she never paced.

"What's wrong, sweet?"

Her glance is worried, her eyes too large in her face. I roll out of bed and hug her from behind, resting my chin on the top of her head.

"We're a team. Tell me."

She shakes her head, wiggling me as she does.

"I've thought all night and can't think of a way out of this predicament. I've crawled all over the Internet on the pad I brought from home. There are no exceptions. There are laws that address black market males. They're to be welcomed to a Newcomer facility and given the choice of being vetted, then they're to find a mate through the proper channels, or be given an all-expense-paid trip home."

"That's it. The women who explained those rules to you weren't lying. I would need to have already registered with an agency. It's too late for them to even consider letting me be your mate."

"There must be something in there about extenuating circumstances."

She shakes her head. "I couldn't find anything."

"We can run, right? Find a place to hide. If not the River of No Return, maybe somewhere else."

"It's a one-world government. Everyone on the planet has to abide by the same rules."

"Then we go with my idea. Zorn is close. We'll find him, then travel back to Draal. I'll take care of you there."

She looks sad, her eyes downcast, avoiding mine. I understand. I'm asking her to leave everything she knows, all the people she holds dear. I've already resigned myself to her refusal to accompany me to Draal when she says, "Okay. Let's go."

"That would make me the happiest male in the galaxy, Lumina, but I won't hold it against you if you change your mind. It would be a big step."

"We've found each other, Zoriss. I'm not letting you go, no matter the cost."

We pack and leave the hotel, then follow the link I feel with my brother. He's happy, so our channel feels wide open.

We drive for hours, but I keep getting my signals wrong. We travel northwest and just when I think we're close, I feel him to the southeast. We've corrected our course three times, but it always turns out wrong.

He's putting off a strong signal that seems to get more powerful with every mile we travel.

Lumina's driving. "You're sure this is right?" she asks as she hovers toward a motel that looks similar to the one we stayed in last night.

"I'm pretty certain."

"We're back in what used to be called Idaho. The one-world government changed the name years ago to New Lillianna, but Idahoans are a stubborn lot and we all still refer to it by its old name. The dingy motel never changed its signage. It's proudly named East-West Idaho," she explains.

We hover to a stop and rather than further inspect the ramshackle one-story hotel, my eyes are drawn to a van with a picture of a naked man emblazoned on the side. One leg is cocked, the knee pointing skyward so his thigh covers his cocks, but he's naked all the same.

"The No Shame Sex Toys van looks conspicuously out of place, don't you think?" she asks, slightly shocked. "I'll be willing to bet my meager life savings they're not from around here."

Her tone is light and joking, but I'm not paying close attention. Zorn is here! I have no doubt.

"I don't know your customs. How can I find Zorn without getting us in trouble?"

"I think all we'll need to do is ask, Captain."

We exit the hover and she grabs my hand and pulls me toward the office. I don't know why she's expecting anyone to help us. My only frame of reference is the mean female who called me a wog last night.

"What's a wog?" I ask right before she opens the door.

"A derogatory term for you."

Why did I bother asking? It was obvious.

She drags me into the small office and asks, "Seen any other Draalians around lately? We were supposed to meet friends here."

"Friends? They could be brothers."

Emotion slams into me so hard I can't swallow. I've never been separated from my clutchmate this long.

"Which room?"

"Shameless," the brown-haired female replies, "I mean No Shame. Room seventeen."

"Thanks."

"Hey! Want a room?" she calls after us before we're out the door.

"We'll be back," Lumina tells her. "I'll wait in my hover if you want," she offers as I practically run toward room seventeen.

"Why?"

"Privacy? Do you want to be alone with your brother for a moment?"

It crosses my mind that Zorn could be in trouble, perhaps I need a weapon. But I don't feel anything but happiness from him. And . . . arousal?

"We'd better knock," I caution.

Zorn knows it's me. I'm assaulted by his joy and connection. The door flings open before I can rap on the door.

There he is. My brother. Naked. As I visually inspect him, making sure he's unharmed, it's hard to miss the fact that he's erect and there's a naked female in here with him. Well, I'm not certain she's naked. By the way she's clutching the bedspread around her, her bare shoulders peeking out above it, I would wager a bet she is.

"You met a female!" we both say at the same time. He looks Lumina up and down.

"Zorn, this is my . . ." I pause for a moment, not knowing what her signifier should be. We've never discussed it. I don't want to overstep my bounds. "Lumina. She's agreed to return to Draal with me."

Polite greetings are exchanged and my brother motions for his female to join us in our cluster at the door. "This is my love, Annora."

"So nice to meet you. I'll be out in a minute." She grabs clothes from where they look like they've been hurriedly thrown on the floor and scurries into the bathroom.

Lumina

"Sit," Zorn motions to the rickety table in the corner. It has two chairs. I slide into one as the two brothers hug each other. You'd think reptilians would be voted the least likely race to display public affection, but they aren't embarrassed to embrace each other. It is so loving, so heartfelt, it brings tears to my eyes.

"You had me worried," Zorn tells him.

"Until yesterday I'd assumed you were safely on Draal," Zoriss says.

Annora slips out of the bathroom, now fully dressed. She lingers a few feet away from the action, appearing to take in the reunion with as much joy as me.

Her gaze catches mine and she says, "He was worried sick about your male."

She acknowledged that he's my male! I like her already.

"And Zoriss couldn't wait to find your male."

I run to the hover to get what's left of the junk food I bought before I started my road trip. We sit around the table, both of us women on our guys' laps. While we eat chocolate and relieve our stress, we catch up.

I can't help but notice that Zorn's gaze is glued to Annora's hands as she brings the chocolate confections from the table to her mouth. If I didn't know better, by the look on his face, I'd think he had a boner. Well, a couple of them. There's something about her eating that seems like a private joke between them. A very sexy private joke.

"Give us an update about your time on Earth," Zoriss says as he looks from Annora to Zorn and back again.

"Well," Annora starts off, "I think it would be fair to say we got off to a rocky start."

Zoriss and I exchange furtive glances, then I minutely inspect the chipped table under my fingers. I doubt their rocky start could be any rockier than ours.

"My mom bought Zorn on the black market." She has the decency to look embarrassed as she shrugs. I don't worry too much because it's obvious they resolved whatever happened at the beginning of their relationship.

"She locked him in a cage in our guest house, then locked me in the house with him."

"Rocky." Zorn nods as if his one-word answer explains everything.

"I'll be the first to admit that I found Draalians unattractive," Annora says as she wipes a non-existent smudge of food from Zorn's mouth with her thumb, then gives him a magma-hot look that promises 'later'.

"Repulsive," Zorn corrects without rancor.

"No offense, Zoriss." She glances his way for a moment, then adds, "Draals? Totally repulsive." She stops her narrative and kisses Zorn soundly on the lips. The look in her eyes is so soft and loving it makes me wonder what happened to change her repulsion into love because that's certainly her emotion now. "We decided to make the best of it and agreed he wouldn't kill me and I wouldn't force him to eat any family pets."

Seriously?

"That didn't last long until, you know, torpor."

Zoriss shoots his brother a concerned look.

"I'm fine," Zorn reassures him.

"Then we escaped together in the No Shame van with a bunch of malfunctioning sexbots in the back," Zorn adds as he puts his arm around Annora and tucks her even closer to him.

"No shit?" I ask. Malfunctioning sexbots? Sounds like it might have provided some comic relief.

"We were on a cross-country race to find you, Zoriss. I even had to pretend I was one of the bots in the back of the van to get through a check stop," Zorn smirks. "I got your signal a few times, but it wasn't strong."

"I was at the bottom of a deep crevasse," Zoriss tells him. "And close to torpor myself."

"When we lost your signal completely, we wound up at Yellowstone Park, saw Old Faithful, got accosted by a lunatic fringe bunch of anti-aliens, and Zorn got abducted," Annora explains.

"Yeah," he says wryly. "What are the odds of being abducted twice?"

"How I tracked him down and saved him is a story for another day," Annora says with a satisfied smile. "Although it involved getting shot." She points to her shoulder. "Don't worry. I'm fine."

"So, in other words, everything went smoothly. And during all that boring downtime you guys . . .?" I point back and forth between them. "Fell in love?"

"Annora is my life," Zorn says without hesitation or prompting, then shoots her a panty-melting look of affection.

"Awww." So freaking sweet. I like this guy.

When Annora prompts for my story, I start my explanation with a long, "Uhhh . . ." How am I going to cop to the fact that Zoriss was a complete asshole to me until I fell down the cliff and almost died?

"I was completely contemptible to Lumina the whole time we were stuck at the bottom of the steep canyon," Zoriss explains even though it puts him in a horrible light. "She saved my life more than once and gave me her body heat and I called her despicable and mocked her."

"You mocked me?" I ask, offended. I knew he was scornful. I didn't know he was insulting. Well, now that I recall his degrading tone of voice, I guess I did know.

"Relentlessly. I have no excuse." He gives an almost imperceptible shrug, but doesn't minimize his behavior.

"Well, in his defense," I chime in, "my translator didn't work, so I didn't know what he was saying and he thought I just wanted him for his cock and his sperm."

Annora gives a whoop of laughter. "Don't you?" She leans over and gives Zorn a long kiss full of tongue.

"Umm . . . yeah?" I admit. "Although, regarding the sperm, the scientists haven't figured out how to help human/Draalian embryos carry to term. I did a deep Internet search. They're close, though."

"So," Annora peers at Zoriss, "something must have happened to change you from thinking she's despicable to looking at her like you can't wait to get to your own room so you can get it on."

"I saw the error of my ways," he explains. "It just took me a few days to get over my rage at being abducted and lying paralyzed but conscious for the three months we were in stasis. It was only then I could admit to myself how amazing this female is."

"You were conscious the whole time?" Zorn asks, his eyes wide in disbelief. He can only stare at Zoriss with his mouth open as Zoriss gives a tight affirmative nod, a look of bitter suffering on his face.

I can't even begin to imagine what that would be like. Mind going ninety miles an hour and unable to move? I'd be certifiably crazy, by the end of one month let alone three. What an amazingly strong male I have. The reasons for his anger and resentment become even more understandable.

We give a few more details about the past week including the horrid woman at the East-West Idaho motel, and then all the smiles fade from our faces.

"Not to bring a crashing end to the party, but the facts are clear," I say. "These guys are here illegally. We've looked into it, unless we were in line with a matchmaking service already, the guys can't be matched with us. They'd have to meet someone new who had already paid her fee and been vetted. I guess the only choice we have is for them to choose another Earth female or for all of us to go back to their home planet. I agreed that after we found you, I'd accompany Zoriss to Draal."

My heart squeezes. I'm the only family my mom has. I don't want to leave her, or my veterinary practice. I may not be raking in the credits, but I love what I do and I'm an integral part of the community.

"Uh," Annora's face squeezes in pain. It must be how I look when I have to tell a pet-mom that it's time to put her pet-kid to sleep. "I *am* in line."

Zorn, Zoriss, and I whip our heads to stare at her.

"Yeah, the day my mom shoved me into our guest cottage, I'd just received word that I could begin attending mixers at the agency I'd applied to. I'll admit, Draalians weren't on my list, but I think Zorn and I meet the criteria you just described. Once we get Zorn registered at the Windy City facility, it will just be a formality for us to register as mates."

My face feels hot, as a pang of jealousy flies through me. Staring at the couple across from me, I want the best for them, I do.

They're obviously in love. But I want to stay on Earth with my guy too.

A long conversation ensues, with us discussing all the options. The brothers have a heart-to-heart about how they feel about being on different planets. One thing we all agree on is that the brothers can't be separated. They both say they'll feel like they lost a limb if they're not together.

"My mom is feeling contrite. Well, more than that, she's feeling guilty as hell," Annora reveals. "I mean, she imprisoned him in a cage and locked me in the cottage. Zorn's decision not to press charges, and mom's heartfelt regret, as well as her connections, mean she will not face prosecution. I'm going to call her and see what she can do for you. If strings can be pulled, she's the one who can do it."

"I can connect her to the agency I used," her mom offers as soon as Annora explains the situation over comms. "You know I'd do anything to make up for all the trouble I caused. I'll contact you back as soon as I get through to them."

Her mom, Grace, owns one of the largest sex toy companies in the world. I guess money and power talk, because not half an hour later she calls back and tells us on speaker, "I talked to the CEO of Heavenly Matches, the service I used to purchase Zorn. Let me apologize again, I'm so sorry. She runs a little off-the-books enterprise she reserves for her friends. Her aunt is high up in the Repopulation Initiative and they work together to arrange paperwork for a select few who need mates fast."

You can feel her excitement from a thousand miles away when she says, "My friend can slide you into her program seamlessly," she announces. "The brothers will have legitimate papers and both you girls can step right up and choose them."

I feel as if a million-pound weight is lifted from my shoulders. After letting out a happy squeal, I turn, squeeze Zoriss as tightly as I can, and kiss him. I can barely see. Tears of relief are flooding my eyes.

"For one-hundred thousand credits," Grace adds.

My mouth flops open as my heart stutters in my chest.

"Thanks, Grace," I manage to grit out. "Thanks so much for your effort." My headache comes back with a vengeance and my eyes are so full of tears I can't see at all. My elation turned to devastation in a heartbeat. "I could never come up with that amount of money."

My mind is whirling with all the permutations of options for the four of us. If the clutchmates have to stay together, this leaves only one option—a one-way trip to Draal.

"I feel responsible for this whole mess," Grace admits. "I'm a bit strapped for cash, what with the new factory in Parasack and paying the fee for Zorn. But I could come up with half."

"Wow. How generous. Thank you, that's so very kind, but I'm sorry, I couldn't—"

"Yes. You *can* accept. I, for one, don't want to go to Draal, and we can't separate the clutchmates," Annora says. "So I have a stake in getting you two legally mated. I can pitch in twenty-five thousand. Can you come up with the other twenty-five?"

"I—" I almost refuse again. I don't like taking charity, and that's what this is. I could never pay them back.

As if she read my mind, Annora says, "It would be a gift, not a loan. I want you two to be happy, and I want the guys to stay together. And I like Earth and don't want to leave. So, can you, Lumina? Can you come up with twenty-five thousand?"

Can I? I think out loud, "I have around thirteen thousand in my savings."

"She was saving for a Draalian," Zoriss says with a warm smile on his face. "She says it was her fondest desire." He shakes his head sadly when he says, "I have nothing to add. Zorn and I spent our income paying off family for the money they loaned us toward mom's medical treatment."

It makes me sad to think his society doesn't have free healthcare for everyone.

"Okay," Annora says in an enthusiastic cheerleader voice. "You need twelve grand. Can you do it?"

My mind starts working like the world's fastest computer. Mom has nothing, but the city of Crentin loves me. I've been saving pet lives, making house calls, and doing favors for people there my whole life.

"We were in that isolated cave for a while. What day is it?"

"October 29."

"I have an idea." I pause a moment, as all of a sudden everything falls into place. Can I do it? I look at my Zoriss. He offered to leave everything he's ever known to stay on Earth with me. Can I find twelve grand?

"We're going to get a good night's sleep," I inform everyone as I stand and pull Zoriss out of the chair. "You two go back to Windy City. I'll let you know by midnight on the 31st if I've come up with the credits. Come on, babe. We've got a lot to do."

~.~

It's been a whirlwind since Zoriss and I left Annora and Zorn's room in that motel two days ago. They're hovering back to Windy City, and we're pulling into my hometown of Crentin.

Most towns gave up the practice of celebrating Halloween decades ago. There were dark times when AD-90 hit, and a lot of simple joys went by the wayside. It just seemed disrespectful, after 99.9% of the men on the planet died in the same year, to celebrate anything, especially something so frivolous as an old pagan holiday.

Eventually, we all pulled up our big girl panties and restructured the planet as well as our lives. Despite the lack of men, women decided to make the best of the untenable situation. My home-town of Crentin didn't celebrate the festival back in the dark times, but eventually we reclaimed the celebration—with a vengeance.

The town is small, with just over a thousand hearty inhabitants. The surrounding area, including farms and ranches, brings the population to more than double that, and everyone comes to town for the Halloween parade and fair.

I'd already paid for my booth like I do every year. Everyone in the area knows who I am. I'm the only vet for miles, but it's good P.R. and, as my mentor taught me, "it's the cost of doing business."

This year, however, the booth won't consist of the usual folding table, chair, and a box of business cards everyone immediately throws away. This year will be different—thanks to my mom.

While Zoriss and I have been hovering here, she's been doing all the footwork. She hasn't complained. She knows how high the stakes are.

We arrive just in time to catch the parade. Main Street—well, the only street, really—is lined with people. Everyone in the county is here, either performing in the parade or watching it.

"Want to watch?" I ask Zoriss, my eyebrow lifting happily. Although we literally don't know where we'll be tomorrow, I can't hide the smile that stretches across my face. This parade, this town, has been an integral part of my life. These people are one big extended family.

The feeling is bittersweet. Whether or not this ends the way we hope, this will be the last Halloween parade I'll watch in Crentin.

After parking the hover, we enjoy the festivities. Zoriss isn't just the only Draalian most people in town have seen, he's the only alien they've seen. He's met with mostly fascination and just a dash of fear, but he seems more focused on the parade than the stares being directed his way.

Teens on horseback aren't just walking down the street. They're threading the needle at a lope as two lines of riders on either side of the street cross over to the other side, one in front of the other requiring precision so they don't end up in a spectacular crash.

Although most people in town are casting Zoriss sidelong glances, his eyes are wide in that gorgeous reptilian face as he watches in fascination at a culture vastly different from his own.

"Those beasts are big compared to the young females."

"They're docile animals, and well trained."

"Beautiful!"

"Horses," I inform him, more intrigued by him than the animals.

A display of vintage tractors follows the riders. I've never liked this part of the parade. It reminds me of how things used to be when all vehicles were powered by non-renewable energy. And it stinks. I don't even know how they keep these things running, but many of the farmers love to show off their antique equipment.

After the marching band from the local school plays "Lilium the Beautiful", the Grand Mistress of Ceremonies gets on the loud-speaker and invites everyone to the Town Hall lawn for the fair.

"You're sure this is acceptable behavior?" Zoriss asks, still not believing I'll be okay with what's coming next.

"We need the money. The question is, are *you* going to be okay with it?" I ask. He was absolutely positively not on board when I first proposed this. He said it would be scandalous on Draal, and disrespectful to me, so at first, he firmly refused. I kept repeating that old quote "desperate times call for desperate measures" and he reluctantly agreed.

I snag his brother's coat from the hover, and we follow the crowd to City Hall. Zoriss said they both had coats like this thick crimson one with gold piping. It's his military dress uniform, and it looks it. He escaped the pirate ship naked, but his brother arrived in his and was kind enough to loan it to us.

The way it looks with the knee-high black boots his brother also loaned him makes me want to drag him to the nearest private room and have my way with him. There's something about a male in uniform. But we're on a more important mission.

There's my booth, in the same spot it's been for the last eight years. It looks nothing like it has in the past, though. My mom did a great job.

"There's mom!" I say as I thread my arm through his and hurry toward her.

Mom's known about my "Drool over Draalians" fixation since it started. For the last three years, she hasn't even given me any presents for birthdays and holidays. She just transfers credits directly into my Draalian account.

"Oh my. He's more handsome than you described," she gushes loudly when we're still yards away. "Hi, Zoriss!" she says, her voice friendly and open.

He approaches her stiffly, not wanting to break any unwritten protocol, but mom won't have any of that. She pulls him into a warm hug and whispers something into his ear. It's so hard to tell on his reptilian features, but I think he's embarrassed. Scales don't pinken, but by the dip of his chin and the way he's avoiding her eyes, I'm dying to find out what she said.

"All right, Emerson," he says, calling her by her first name. My Draalian captain is shy!

As if she read my mind, she says, "I told him to call me by my first name and that I want to get his first kiss." When my eyes flare open, she corrects, "Of the day!"

When it's apparent Zoriss is readying himself to kiss her right this moment, mom says, "Not here," and pulls him to my booth.

She enlisted some of her friends to help her construct it. It consists of two sturdy wooden uprights about seven feet tall that hold a six-inch-wide board at table height. At the top, the stanchions hold a crimson fabric banner that proclaims, "Kiss a

Draalian" in gold lettering. Below it in smaller letters, it says, "by Donation."

"I'm the first," my mom yells. As if it was all choreographed, half the women in town hurry to form a line behind her.

My Draalian, his top teeth biting his bottom lip in the sexiest display of bashfulness I've ever seen, steps behind the booth and squares his shoulders. He has no idea how erotic those fangs of his are. If he knew, he'd pull them back into his mouth. I think those fangs might have enticed any women who were on the fence about their kiss, because more of them crowd into the back of the line.

Mom gives him a chaste kiss on the cheek, and I can almost feel his relief. I hurry closer and manage the exchange of credits.

"Thanks, mom. For all your help. And this donation? So generous."

"I just want my daughter to be happy. Is he as nice as he seems?" She's beaming.

I take a deep breath and once and for all relegate those first few shitty days to the back of my mind.

"Yes, mom. He is."

I manage the flow of money into my account as Zoriss manages not to damage anyone with his fangs.

"I'm paying good money for this, Draalian," Edora McPhee demands, "I want some tongue." She's one of the oldest women in Crentin. Even her wrinkles have wrinkles. I'm about to intervene, but Zoriss's expression tells me he's got this.

"And tongue you shall receive, Ma'am."

"Oh, this one's polite," she says, nodding to her friends at the tail of the line.

Instead of leaning forward, though, Captain takes half a pace back and does his tongue trick, allowing the two halves to twine around each other, first one way and then the other. He's pegging her with a serious stare.

She places her hand on her chest and tears fill her eyes. I always thought of her as an old woman. She's been ancient since I was a kid. Mom leans in and says, "She was one of the last on Earth to have a mate, Lumina. I think he's helping her remember she used to be a sexual woman many years ago."

I'm dumbfounded.

"He didn't have to do that, Lumina. He just gave her a gift."

The older woman totters over to me, and I can see the wetness in her rheumy eyes. I'm shocked by the generosity of the amount she wants to transfer into my account. "I was saving for a rainy day, dear. I can't imagine anything more important to spend it on."

"Thank you, Ms. McPhee."

Shortly after two, I check the balance in my account and see we've exceeded our goal by a few thousand credits.

Before the next woman steps up for her kiss, I ask Zoriss to stand me on the horizontal bar that keeps his patrons from reaching in and attacking him. When he realizes it's none too sturdy, he keeps a firm hold on my hips.

"I want to thank all of you for your support," I shout to the crowd. "I love this town and I'm so proud of you for coming through for us. I want you to know how much Zoriss and I appreciate this. We've met our goal, so we don't need any more of your—"

"Shut up, young lady," Lavinia Rose says from her place near the back of the line. "I want my fucking kiss."

I must admit, it's shocking to hear the hundred and twenty-year-old woman talk like that.

I hear a lot of grumbles. Many "Me too's," gather volume as the sentiment moves up the line.

"Uh . . ."

Mom steps forward. "I propose we let them keep the next five thousand to start them on their wedded journey and put any additional money into the City Renovations Fund."

"I agree," shouts Lavinia.

That settles it. The kissing continues until I can barely stand to see my male's lips on another female. His gaze flies to mine, a desperate look in his eyes. Since I became an expert at reading his body language when we were in the cave, I'm pretty sure he's at the "If I have to kiss one more female I'm going to make you pay" stage.

"Thank you, everyone," I shout as I snag him around the waist and pull him out from behind the booth. "We've got to get on the road." I don't feel bad in the least when I realize all the women in line were simply coming back for seconds. The nerve!

I tell mom I'll meet her back at my house in ten minutes, but Zoriss interrupts.

"I want to try that," he says, his gaze flicking to a booth on the other side of the lawn. "I've been watching whenever I had a free minute. It was easier than looking at the long line of females waiting in line to kiss me. What is it?"

I follow his gaze and see the bobbing for apples booth. Frankly, I never understood the appeal of this particular tradition. I still don't see the allure of half-drowning yourself, dislocating your jaw, and ruining a perfectly good hair day to wind up with an apple that someone else has already taken half a bite out of.

"Bobbing for apples? Really?"

"I'm going to be very good at it," he proclaims. Once we arrive, he watches a few other participants, asks what the winning time is so far, and gives a curt nod of his head.

This gives me a little taste of the pre-Earth Zoriss. I like him. Supremely confident, willing to try new things, optimistic. Funny, I have no doubt he *is* going to be very good at it.

After unbuttoning his thick coat and handing it to me, he kneels next to the tub, gives me a wink and a smile, and launches into action the moment the woman running the booth says, "Go."

I have just enough time to notice that almost everyone on the lawn has wandered over to see the reptilian alien who was heretofore wearing a thick coat on a balmy day, stick his head in a barrel of cold water.

His hairless head lifts up out of the water less than twenty seconds later, a huge smile on his face and one ripe, juicy apple impaled on one of his fangs.

"That was the best time of the day so far. Probably the best time ever, but I don't know if you should win," Sydney Thompson says as she offers him a towel. "I think your . . . Draalianess gives you an unfair advantage."

"That's okay," he shrugs, still smiling as he pulls the fruit off his fang. "What do you do with these things anyway?"

I grab the towel from him to catch some drips sluicing down the back of his neck. "Eat them."

Reptiles mostly eat meat, but Draals can eat other Earth food items. I don't think he likes Earth food, though, because other than the nutrition bars we shared, I haven't seen him eat much other than the awful crickets and mealworms he ate in the cave. Luckily, he does that in the other room because it makes me want to hurl.

He takes a big bite of his apple, and his eyes fly open, then the lids slam closed as he moans, making a sound eerily close to the very satisfied noise he makes during sex.

"Wow," he exclaims around his second bite.

We make a good team—he eats and I make judicious use of the towel to keep the juice from running down his chin.

He charms Sydney Thomson out of another apple when he tells her it's the most delicious apple he's ever tasted, and we stride to the hover as he munches happily away.

A few minutes later we've rendezvoused with mom at my apartment. This is going to be the hard part.

I've decided to leave most of my things here. My furniture was mostly donated by extended family and friends years ago. It's not worth transporting across the country.

Mom and Zoriss sit on the couch and get acquainted as I walk through my apartment touching the things I've accumulated over a lifetime. It hits me like a lightning bolt that there's nothing I'm going to miss.

I cast my gaze in his direction and drink in the sight of him. In just this short amount of time, he's become the most important thing in my life. I throw clothes, toiletries, and a few mementos into several bags and join the two people I love most in the world in the living room.

After pulling a chair in front of Zoriss and my mom so one of each of my knees is touching one of theirs, I grab a hand in each of mine.

"I couldn't have pulled this off without you, mom. The kissing booth? Well done. And contacting Dr. Perri Thompson from Lanaquan to see if she wanted to use my office two days a week to see my patients and pay me a small percentage for the first two years? Wow! That was brilliant. Between that and the extra seven grand we made at the kissing booth, we're going to be fine in Windy City.

"I hate to go, but the guys have to be together and Annora can't relocate. Her corporate offices are there.

"It just leaves one little loose end." My eyes are sparkling with unshed tears. How do I gather my nerve to ask my mom to leave the only town she's ever known, one filled with people who love her, in order to follow me halfway across the country? I guess I'll do it the same way I asked Zoriss to stay here with me and leave the life he loved halfway across the galaxy.

"The loose end of the Draalian sexbot?" she asks innocently, as if she didn't know where this conversation was really going.

"Well, um, it *is* worth money," I answer.

"I was thinking of donating it." She pauses for effect, then says, "To Edora McPhee."

When Zoriss cocks his browridge at me I ask, "Wondering about the sexbot or Ms. McPhee?"

"Both." He stands. "Where's the bot?"

"Prominently displayed in my bedroom, honey." My head sinks into my palms.

He stalks into my room and I know when he sees it by the hiss of displeasure I hear from the other room.

"Shit," I mumble under my breath.

"Shit is right," he says. Damn, when will I remember that their hearing is superhuman? "You paid good money for thissss?"

"He's really mad when he starts hissing," I whisper to mom.

"Not mad. Insulted." He charges into the room holding the bot by the back of the neck.

When I see them together like that, I begin chuckling, then my laughter becomes louder.

"Are you . . . jealous?" I ask, incredulous. Now that they're in the same room, it's absurd how much I paid for that thing. First of all, it's nowhere near the height or bulk of the real deal. And the penises? Don't even get me started. It's pathetic.

"That nice older female needs this bot," he agrees as he motions me out of my chair and sets it on the seat. He sits on the couch, pulls me onto his lap, then suddenly appears worried, his eyes rounded as his glance darts toward mom. "Is this appropriate?"

"Your love is adorable," mom says, a wide smile on her face. "So, when are you going to invite me to move to Windy City? I think at my age it would be good to try something new."

"You're terrific, mom," I tell her with relief. She knew my request was coming, she just beat me to it.

We spend a few minutes discussing details. She's going to stay in Crentin for a while, dispatching my things as well as hers and putting her house up for sale. We agree that Zoriss and I will go to Windy City and get settled, then look for a place for her.

"It won't be too intrusive to have your mate's mother so close?" mom asks Zoriss. Her tone is light, but I can hear the apprehension in her voice. The last thing she wants is to interfere.

His head snaps back in surprise. "Emerson, Draals are matrilineal. Females are venerated. You would be an honored part of our new family." He places her hand between his and squeezes. "My mother passed away a few years ago. Zorn and I will consider you, my beloved Lumina, Annora, and her mother to be our new family."

Wow! If I wasn't in love with him before, I would be after that.

"I guess it's fair to say you two haven't given much thought to your mating ceremony?" Mom asks.

Zorris's eyes widen in what, surprise? Have I been living in an alternate universe for the last few days? Does he not want to marry me?

"You don't want to mate me?" I ask, my voice a shocked whisper.

He touches behind his left ear. That must be where his translator is located. "Am I understanding correctly?"

"I assume we're going to be mated. That's what all of this has been about, right?" I ask.

"Yes." He nods happily. "Mated."

"But, you don't want a ceremony?" I ask, leaning forward as I wait for an answer.

His eyes slide to mom. "On Earth are these things so openly discussed? I guess it's like the sexbot?"

I've recently learned his embarrassed expression, and he's wearing it now. Although it's adorable on him, eyes downcast, lips pressed together, I take the hint.

"I'll get back to you on that, Mom."

"Okay. I hope you'll wait until I can be there for it."

Zoriss sounds like he just choked on his own spit.

10

Zoriss

After that awkward conversation with Emerson, I helped Lumina go through her house one more time, then carried her belongings to her hover. She was nostalgic about leaving things behind, yet didn't want to take a lot of them with her.

"I'm starting a new life," she said with a happy smile. "So . . . the mating ceremony? Care to tell me what that means in your culture?" she asks with a provocative smile after we hover away.

"It's an extremely private and personal ceremony that two partners share. I couldn't believe your mother mentioned watching. Otherwise, I thought she was a wonderful person."

"It happens in the bedroom?"

"Usually. You'd like it somewhere else?" His eyes leave the road for a moment and flash to me. "On Earth, it's done in . . . public?" I don't recall them covering this in my indoctrination during stasis.

"You are so handsome when you're scandalized," she says as she reaches over and pats my thigh. "I might just have to dream up more ways to shock you."

Then she explains that on Earth the ceremony is fully clothed and performed in front of family and friends. When I give her a hint of what the Draalian mating ceremony entails, her mouth pops open in surprise. She asks a few more questions, but the aroma of her arousal fills the vehicle.

"When, uh, when would a couple perform this Draalian mating ceremony?" she asks as we enter the outskirts of the largest city I've seen since I arrived on Earth. The downtown welcomes us with a huge, metallic arch.

"We'll conduct the ritual when you're ready."

She's quiet for a while.

"Having second thoughts?" I ask.

"No. Just counting up the miracles, Captain. If you're ready, I'd like to do it tonight."

My cocks kick in unison. "I'm ready, Love. Do you think you could find lodgings that are nicer than the East-West Idaho motel?"

"That can be arranged."

Two hours later, we're in our room in a nice hotel. It's clean, and I have no worries that the proprietor is watching on a hidden camera. We stopped to buy proper clothing, and I've taken my ritual bath.

I asked Lumina to download Draalian drum music, and it's playing in the background while she is in the bathroom.

I'm on my knees, in a private moment with my God, giving thanks. I grew up with the certainty I would never have this. I didn't even allow myself to dream of this day, knowing it would never come.

From a young age, every Draalian knew the dire consequences of global warming on our population. Our family wasn't one of the few that was rich enough to provide a dowry for a female. Zorn and I had no hope of mating and became content to spend the rest of our lives in the military.

Having this, with a female I love, is the best thing to ever happen to me. My heart bursts with happiness.

Lumina emerges from the bathroom in the simple white dress we just bought her. I'm wearing white slacks and a tunic.

"Join me, Love." I motion to the floor, and she kneels facing me. I hold her hands, gaze into her lovely blue eyes, and speak from my soul.

"We've spoken of all the miracles that brought us together. I'm the luckiest male in the galaxy to have the sweetest, most generous, and definitely the most beautiful female forgive my numerous imperfections and agree to be my beloved lifemate.

"I promise to cherish you, try to put your needs before mine, and take care of you to the best of my ability. I love you with all of my heart."

I search my soul for a moment and realize I've said everything I need to say.

"Just speak from the heart, Love." I squeeze her hand, then realize that isn't good enough, so I bring it to my lips and kiss her palm.

My heart clenches when I see the luminous look of love in her eyes.

"I dreamed of this day, even though I thought it would never come. You're my soulmate, Zoriss. The universe conspired to get us here because we were meant to be together. I love you."

She looks shy and maybe a little worried. I glossed over most of the details about the mating ceremony. I wasn't certain how it would work between a Draalian and a human.

Lumina

We've had sex dozens of times since we met. He tells me this will be different, and special.

Scooting on his knees to get closer to me, he smooths my hair from my face and holds my cheeks in his palms.

"Listen to the drums, Love. It's two heartbeats. Always two heartbeats."

He's right. I can hear it. No matter how fast or slow, or whatever other instruments might intertwine with them, it's the two beating drums that take center stage.

His mouth covers mine, and he kisses me chastely over and over in time with the drums.

"I love you, Lumina. Are you ready?"

I'm not even sure what I'm ready for. I guess I'm ready for anything. "Yes."

"I lead. You follow. When we're done, we'll be lifemates. Forever," he tells me, then rises and pulls me to my feet.

We stand, kissing for long moments. At first, they're just soft kisses. They punctuate the beautiful words we just shared with each other. Then his tongue slips between my lips. He delves into my mouth as the cool of his slim tongue strokes my warm one.

My nipples prick in excitement, and I feel his cocks press against my belly as he scoots my body closer to his with his hand on my ass.

"I'm going to love you as you were meant to be loved," he breathes against my lips, then nibbles them.

I slide my palms from where they're lodged at his shoulders, down the steel cables of his back muscles, and let them settle on the curve of his fine ass. Pressing him closer, I pay attention to the length and girth of his primary as it pulses against me in the rhythm of the pounding drums.

The sweet ceremony of a moment ago is a distant memory as his movements become wilder. His hands roam and he makes deep noises from the back of his throat until he can't keep up the pretense of civility anymore and yanks my dress over my head.

He gives me a sensuous smile when he finds me naked under the dress, even though those were his explicit instructions before I took my shower.

"Gorgeous," he says in English, although it sounds more like 'jus' because his mouth is busy kissing a path down the sensitive column of my neck toward my nipple.

The white pants and tunic he wears are soft muslin. They're so thin they barely contain the prodigious bulges in his pants, but I want them off. I want us skin to skin. When I try to pull his top up, though, he shakes his head, lifts me, and deposits me on the bed.

I can almost hear the war going on in his head as he argues with himself over pouncing on me right now or continuing his leisurely pace. I know which side won the war when he tears his shirt over his head, shucks out of his pants and kicks them out of the way.

He prowls up my body, nipping and biting with his flat front teeth. Pulling out the big guns, he slides down to my ankles, then skims up the inside of my leg with the sharp points of his two fangs. He's on a collision course with my sex, but veers at the last moment, pulls his head up, and places a sweet kiss on my mons.

"Do that again," I order, and he does, mirroring what he just did on the other leg. His teeth are so sharp I lift my head to see if there are two parallel red lines racing up my leg, but no, the skin is intact. My self-control, however, is in shreds as I desperately want to feel his tongue between my legs.

He's not in a compliant mood, though, because he slides back to the foot of the bed, crouches there, and makes a slow journey back up the inside of my leg, this time with his tongue. I can't tear my eyes from the display as that talented blue tongue glides up, the two halves of his tongue painting me with his saliva in precise figure-eights of lust.

"Zorisss!" I love to hiss his name, but I don't want to play. "Stop teasing."

He doesn't spare me a glance, much less comply. He just splits my legs wider, presses his nose into the spot where my thigh meets my torso, and tongues me until I shiver, then writhe, then moan, then beg.

"Please." I can't speak in complete sentences. I want him to read my mind and know what I want.

Finally, he takes pity on me and moves his head a few inches. When both halves of his tongue flick my clit, I clutch the bedspread so hard my nails snag the fabric.

"Yes. Right there," I instruct, even though he obviously knows exactly what he's doing.

The onslaught has begun. Whatever game he was playing before in his attempt to go slow, he's pulled out all the stops now. His tongue is flicking so fast it's like a perpetual motion machine.

My arousal is ramping, my thighs clenching as they tense for their release. Zoriss chooses this moment to hiss. I never knew how snakes made this sound, but it feels like a constant vibration from somewhere in his mouth. It shivers its way down to the ends of the tongue that are stimulating my bundle of nerves.

I'm not sure whether the surprise of the vibration adds to my arousal or whether it's the movement itself, but what he just did detonated my orgasm like setting off a depth charge. My hands leave their perch on the bed and grip his shoulders so hard I know in the back of my mind they're going to leave deep furrows in his scales. At this moment I don't fucking care as every muscle in my body spasms in endless bliss.

He lets me ride the crest of the wave, then doesn't even let me drift fully back to normal before he attacks me again. For a split second I consider asking him to give me a moment, but I immediately think better of it as I'm already well on my way to another release.

This time I get there faster, and the orgasm is even more powerful as he slides first one finger, then a second, into my spasming channel.

Again and again, he takes me to the peak of delight, lets me fall almost back to Earth, then assaults me again. I'm mindless and boneless and can't even think as he provides me with wave after wave of relentless pleasure.

Finally, he stops, lifts his head, and with a satisfied, almost smug look on his face, his blue tongue licks my juices from around his mouth.

"Amazing!" I lie back, not even caring that my pillow wound up on the floor somewhere between orgasm number one and number ten. "We're mated now?"

His answer is a hearty laugh. "We're just getting started."

I reach to fondle one of his cocks. I don't care which one, I just want a feel, but he maneuvers away from my hand, lifts my legs, and places his secondary at my entrance. I'm so wet he slides in easily until he gets to the thicker spot halfway up the shaft. The extra tightness as he pushes in makes me pant with pleasure as it presses against me. Between the girth and the ribbing of his bumps, the feeling is out of this world.

After working himself all the way in, he pistons into me, slowly at first, then faster until we're both groaning with every slap of our flesh. He comes with a loud groan and mine hits just as he is peaking.

"Now we're mated?" I ask.

"Soon, my love."

He's still lodged in my body as he dips to kiss me. Something is different. The expression on his face is more serious, questing, as if what's coming next is going to be the most significant thing either of us has ever done.

"Ready?" he asks quietly, his gaze never leaving mine.

I nod.

He kisses me again, just lip on lip, but the exquisite emotion behind it is as if it's a prayer, a hymn, a supplication.

He makes sure I notice him withdraw his secondary and notch his primary against my core. When our gazes are locked, he presses in. Just as fast as he entered me and pounded to completion a moment ago, this is a slow ride as he takes his time sliding a millimeter at a time, filling me.

His primary is at least as long and thick as his secondary. I feel every delicious inch of him during this penetration. He makes sure I notice every ridge and bump on the long journey. His secondary, still slick with my juices, is now sensuously sliding across my clit.

The drumbeats somehow sound louder, everything seems more urgent, more immediate. My emotions are more keyed up as we both wait for him to fill me to the hilt. Once he does, he slides out again, so slowly it's as if he's consecrating me, as if my vagina is holy ground.

And then he starts pumping into me. Every slap against my flesh is punctuated with a deep grunt, then a sibilant hiss that ricochets around the room.

"Don't come until I say," his voice is soft, but the tone leaves no room for doubt how serious he is.

My orgasm has been building, but I try to suppress it, to tamp it down. Keeping our gazes connected helps. I could fly over the edge any moment if he just said the word.

Dipping his mouth to my ear, he husks, "Count to ten slowly, then come."

Opening his mouth wide, he slides his tongue from my ear, down my neck to my shoulder.

As I say, "Five," he pierces me with his fangs. I scream in pain, but it lasts less than a second as I feel his venom burn along my veins, then all I feel is pleasure. The bliss of moments ago when he made me come over and over again is like a picture of an apple compared to the real thing.

This, this is pleasure most mortals only dream of as my vaginal walls spasm around his primary. Every cell in my body is writhing in bliss, dancing among the stars as I experience satisfaction I never could have dreamed of before.

I feel his hot jets release into me and wish I could look into those beautiful, loving eyes, but mine are rolled so far into the back of my head I'm incapable of sight.

I can't speak, can't grunt, can't even moan in pleasure. I can't move or stroke his back or try to kiss his lips. If my mind were still thinking, I would wonder if I just died, but I know I'm still alive because I feel him next to me.

Now we're mated, Love.

I heard that in my mind, not through my ears.

Can you hear me?

"Yes."

Don't move your lips, mate. Talk to me in your head. This is the Draalian psychic link.

You can hear me? I'm shocked.

He snuggles against me, pulls the covers over us, and says, *Yes.*

I finally muster the energy to open my eyes and look at him.

What Draalian psychic link?

I assumed that's why Earth females wanted males from Draal. It's not common knowledge?

No.

I wasn't sure it would even work with Earth females, so I didn't warn you ahead of time. I guess we both got a happy surprise.

Does this go away?

No.

Do we have to reactivate it from time to time?

No. Uh, yes, he amends. *We have to do this all the time or the link fades.*

"You're lying."

"Yes, I am. It will never go away."

"But we can still do this all the time. Did your venom make my orgasm more powerful?"

"That's what the scientists tell us. They say it's a potent aphrodisiac."

I hug him tight and inspect that beautiful face. Gorgeous blue eyes, interesting scale patterns from scalp to chin, mouth that's perfect for kissing.

"We got lucky, Love," I say caressing his cheek with my palm.

"Yes. Everyone should be lucky enough to be abducted to Earth."

I inspect his face, looking for a trace of sarcasm or irony, but he's serious.

I throw my arms around his shoulders and pull him tight. "We're both lucky indeed."

EPILOGUE

Two years later . . .

Zoriss

I've been both looking forward to this and dreading it. At least this time I know what to expect.

We're back in Crentin for the Halloween Festival. The whole town celebrated the first Crentin female and Draalian male mating in the region.

My lovely mate is laughing and joking with all of her old friends. She's so comfortable here, just like in our home back in Windy City.

It took awhile for her to really enjoy living there. For me, though, by the time we hovered across the country and arrived in the city, I was ready to start my new life there. I hadn't lived on Draal in a long time. My life had been with my clutchmate, and now I was going to have a life with him, his mate, and my own.

At first, I missed the military, partly because I enjoyed many aspects of it, partly because it was all I knew. I never dreamed I'd find a job in my new town so quickly, especially one I'd love more than the army.

For my first year on Earth, Zorn and I were invited to join a task force empowered to hunt pirates and bring them to justice. The force was an elite cadre composed of Earth's three species of aliens along with Earth females. We discovered and dismantled three separate criminal groups that had their tentacles high into the government.

We located many males who were brought here illegally. Many, like Zorn and me, had already found love but were living in hiding without proper documentation.

The Earth Repopulation Organization amended their laws and will allow black-market males to stay with the females of their choice if both parties are willing.

Once a month, Zorn and I lead a discussion group for males like myself who've been stolen and brought here illegally. I testify to the fact that there are options other than rushing back to their home planet. I'm helping in some small way, which makes me feel great.

Although there are still miscreants and pirates making Earth unsafe for immigrants, I chose a safer vocation where I'll be home every night. I've become head of security at one of the mating agencies. Having both broken in—well, Lumina broke in —and broken out of the facility out west, I feel uniquely qualified to enhance security as well as provide the perspective of someone who has left their home planet for something better.

My life is so much better than it was in the Draalian military. I don't have to worry about my safety or that of my brother anymore. Our mates love knowing we'll sleep in the same bed with them every night.

I wasn't sure the females would like the living arrangement we all agreed upon, but it's working better than I'd ever imagined. Annora's mom, Grace, moved into the newly renovated cottage behind the main house, insisting that taking care of the big house had become a burden.

That left the eighteen-room mansion for the four of us. With a few renovations, we redesigned the space to have plenty of privacy for our two families, yet several common rooms to have fun together. We all agree that having just one kitchen and sharing the cooking is the smartest thing we ever could have devised.

Lumina's mom, Emerson, moved into a communal living situation in the heart of Windy City. She shares it with eight women about her age. After living in rural New Lilliana all her life, she tells us she's having the time of her life.

Lumina loves her new practice. She's taking over from a female who is preparing to retire. She's even far enough out in the country that she can continue to treat not just household pets, but some of the large bovines and equines residing outside the city.

When I glance over at her across the Town Hall lawn, she's absentmindedly rubbing her flat belly.

You're doing it again, I tell her.

She immediately knows what I'm talking about and puts her hand on her hip. The look on her face is as guilty as if I caught her breaking into an exclusive alien dating mixer.

You don't have to keep it a secret. Didn't you decide you were going to tell everyone today, anyway? I ask.

Yes.

Her mom knows, of course, and Annora and Zorn. She decided to tell the inhabitants of her old town later today when the Festival is over.

Get your coat on, Captain. It's showtime. She taunts.

She's going to enjoy my misery as I kiss the town's inhabitants all afternoon.

As I stride to the booth, she yells and makes the announcement that the kissing booth is now open for business.

I feel a pang of sadness when I look around and don't see Edora McPhee.

Did Edora McPhee pass away? I ask. I can't imagine she would miss this otherwise. She enjoyed it so much last time I was here.

The grapevine has it that she's so happy with a certain Draalian sexbot she has no use for a real male anymore.

Well, I tell her, *I'm glad you still have use for a real male.* The sweet, happy smile she flashes fills me with love.

Lumina

I watch my mate man-up and pucker up for every female from thirteen to one-hundred-thirty who has hovered here from a hundred miles in every direction.

He's so handsome. I still can't tear my eyes from him, nor can I quit feeling like the luckiest female on this or any planet.

And the baby I'm carrying, how amazing is that? Shortly after our private mating ceremony, the news was full of stories about the breakthrough allowing Draals and humans to conceive and carry to term. Because the hybrids will be born live instead of hatched, they have just as much likelihood of being male as female.

When mom arrived in Windy City, we had a small public double mating ceremony at the mansion. It felt even more special that Zoriss got to share the festivities with his clutchmate. The only non-family member there was Taylor Vale from Antiqua. There wouldn't have been a mating ceremony without her. She met a handsome Draalian at a mixer and they're very close to a mating ceremony of their own.

I honestly don't know who was happier on our mating day, the two couples, or our moms. It makes me sad that so many women, like my mom and Grace and thousands more who are my age, will never have the chance for love like I've found. Maybe life will be better for the next generation.

About a year after my walk down the aisle, the captain and I decided we were ready to expand our family and I started on the medication that would allow this miracle to happen.

I love my new job, mom's happy in Windy City, Annora and I are best friends, and when Zorn and Zoriss hug, their love for each other overflowing, I can't help but hope our children will grow up with that same ability to care deeply for each other.

Zoriss doesn't have to speak through our psychic connection, he just casts his eyes toward me with the same pathetic cry for help as he did two years ago around this same time of day.

This time, out of an abundance of caution, I don't balance on the booth's horizontal board, I just stand in front of it and announce the kissing portion of the festivities is over.

"Thanks for your support. This year's proceeds are going to a fund to help pay local women's fees to the dating agency of their choice." I pause, suddenly feeling shy, but then say, "I'm also pleased to announce that the scientific advances you've all been reading about are true. Zoriss and I will be bringing our youngling to the festivities next year."

I glance around the cheering crowd, most of whom are wiping moist eyes. This is the hope of every human on Earth—we're truly repopulating the planet, one cute little Draalhuman baby at a time.

Earth is fully invested in this repopulation initiative, and it's great to be a part of it, but on a smaller scale, everything is more personal.

When you peel back all the layers, everything is really about family.

By this time next year, we'll have added a little Draalhuman or two to the mix, but right this minute, the most important thing in the world is Captain Zoriss Krine and me—and our love. It's our passionate connection that started it all.

I love you, I tell him, then decide it shouldn't be kept a secret just between us.

"I love you, mate," I say loud enough for everyone on the lawn to hear.

"I love you, too," he responds, an indulgent smile on his face.

"You literally came crashing into my life two years ago, Captain. I didn't know it then, but it's the best thing that ever happened to me."

"Agreed, love, agreed."

DEAR READER

I hope you enjoyed Zoriss and Lumina's story. They had to work hard to reach their happily ever after, didn't they?

Want even more of their story? Sign up here for my FREE NEWSLETTER and get a second epilogue. This one is scorching hot. You can always unsubscribe if you'd like, no hard feelings. If you stick around, you'll get free content, cover reveals, and weekly contests for free stuff.

Don't forget to check out the other Cosmic Kissed books written in the same world from kickass authors.

Inspiration is a weird thing. The ideas for both Zoriss's story and that of his brother, Zorn came barreling at me at the same moment. I couldn't write just one of their stories. It was a fun challenge to write two very different books along the same time-line. Check out Zorn and Annora's story here. Scroll down for a SNEAK PEEK OF THEIR FIRST CHAPTER.

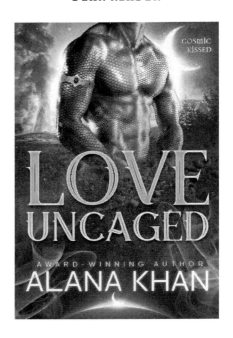

LOVE UNCAGED

CHAPTER 1

Date: 2180

Place: Entering Earth's atmosphere

Zorn

"Wake up, assholes."

What? As I swim up from deep sleep, my thoughts are cloudy and my head is screaming in pain.

"Wake the fuck up. You've slept long enough!"

When my eyes open with effort I realize I'm in a stasis pod. Looking through the clear cover, it's obvious from the filthy ceiling and close proximity of the pod next to me that I'm not on a Draalian military transport. By the length of my fingernails I realize I've been in here for months.

Although my body's stiff and I'm still groggy, the first emotion to come hurtling at me is fear. I shouldn't be here! Although I have no idea where *here* is.

After allowing myself a moment of panicked confusion, I slow my thoughts and move into fact-finding mode. Have I been in a battle I don't remember? Was I captured and transported with my military cohort? Last I recall, my brother and I had just returned to our home planet of Draal for a long-awaited furlough.

"You've been brought to a planet called Earth courtesy of our little pirate operation." The voice is piped into my stasis pod. "Earth can't produce males anymore and the women there are desperate for your cocks and your sperm. We brought you here on a little off-the-books expedition. We get paid. You get mates. They call it pussy. You get all the pussy you want." He laughs crudely. His harsh, grating voice was speaking Draalian.

The muscles in my face harden as I realize one of my own species abducted me and brought me here against my will. They were brash enough to do it to a captain in the planetary army!

"While in stasis we updated your translator chips and down-loaded lessons in their customs into your cerebral cortex. We've already held auctions. You're all bought and paid for."

Unkempt and disorganized armed males bristle through the cabin. From what I see through the clear dome of my pod, it's obvious these males hold no regard for common decency, much less cleanliness and order. They're not even carrying their weapons properly. I wonder how I might escape. There are at least ten of them, and who knows how many of us lie captive in pods. My hand-to-hand skills are good, but I'm no match for ten armed males.

One male slams his fist on top of a pod to my left.

"Fucker! One slipped out."

The pirates mobilize, running toward my left. Laser weapons can't be discharged in a space vessel. One errant blast would pierce the hull and kill all on board. They have to reach the escapee on foot to get close enough to use their stunners.

I watch every step of the drama as the male who woke me shouts and blusters, his microphone still live from his contemptuous welcome speech. Pressing against the top of my pod, it's obvious mine hasn't unlatched yet. The pods must be opening in sequence so we all don't get out at the same moment.

"Fuck! The asshole ejected in an escape pod!"

I can't help but mentally cheer the fellow who was lucky enough to bolt.

"Which stasis pod was he in? Let me check the manifest. Zoriss Krine, a captain in the Draalian planetary army. I wonder where the fuck he thinks he's going. We cannibalized the nav system on our last trip to Earth—that capsule can't be piloted. Wherever he lands—if he survives the landing—he'll still be stranded on this shithole planet."

Zoriss! My clutchmate. My brother. My heart pounds in fear. He escaped in a capsule he can't fly!

One Day Later

Annora

"Mom, I can't remember the last time you were this excited about anything."

"This has consumed me lately. I've had workers renovating the guest house for months and it's finally ready for the big unveiling. I want you to move back here, honey. It's lovely, and as I age it will be nice to have you so close."

"Age my ass, Mom. You're only about to turn sixty. Admit it, you want me close so you can micromanage me."

"You wound me, Annora. I'm the furthest thing from a meddlesome mother. Here we are. Go in first. I want you to see it in all its glory."

"I liked it the way it was, old-fashioned and cozy, but let's see—"

I'm barely over the threshold when the door slams behind me with Mom on the outside and me inside.

"I love you, honey," she says over my wrist-comm.

"What the fuck?" I try to open the front door and can't even turn the doorknob.

"You'll thank me for this later." She's too chickenshit to even have her vid-comm on. I can't see her, only hear her.

"For what?"

I turn from the metal door to inspect the cottage.

"Holy shit, Mom. What have you done?" my voice is low and full of dread. This looks like the beginning of a tragedy of epic proportions.

There's an alien male in the main room. Well, he's not exactly in the main room, he's in a *cage* in the main room.

Human men began dying off ninety years ago and there isn't a man under that age on the planet. Five years ago, human women began an active campaign to repopulate with alien species. Three of which have been approved and are now moving here to mate with a select few women. This male is from Draal. If I can read his snakelike features correctly, he doesn't look any happier about this than I am. There's a muscle leaping on his scale-covered jaw. Eww.

"Mom," I say into my wrist-comm, using my serious-as-a-heart-attack voice, "slavery is illegal. These guys come of their own free will. Why is he in a cage?"

"Your application was going so slowly. I just wanted to hurry things along. I used my contacts to buy him on the black market," she says in the singsong voice she uses when she's anxious.

I try the front door again, then skirt the cage to jiggle the handle of the French doors that open onto the back gardens, then I pound on the door in the kitchen that exits to the side yard. All locked from the outside. My heart is thumping hard against the wall of my chest, my palms are sweating, and my mind is racing as I search for a way out of this fiasco.

"I hear you rattling the knobs. Go ahead, get it out of your system. You'll notice I not only updated the cottage, I installed every conceivable mechanism to keep you inside until you and your Draal decide to mate."

I scrub my face with my hand, then start opening kitchen drawers. No knives, although I don't know what I'd do with one other than hurt my mom if I could get my hands on her.

"Is this about your desire for grandkids, mom? Because as I recall they're not even sure his species is compatible with ours."

"No dear. I watched my parents have a loving relationship my entire childhood. When I was of childbearing age there was no way to have children except through artificial insemination. That's how I got you. And we had a good life. It's just that I want you to have what my parents had, and what I desperately desired my entire life. I want you to have a loving mate."

"This is insane! I'd already applied with Heavenly Mates. I—"

"Why don't you get to know Zorn? The testing says you're 98% compatible."

"Mom, have you lost your mind? You think buying him on the black market and *caging* him will result in a loving relationship? Plus, I didn't want a reptile! I didn't apply for one." I whisper, "They're so repulsive!" Then recall I read somewhere their hearing is amazing. Crap. His blue eyes are staring lasers through me with eat-shit-and-die looks. I wish I hadn't said that. I imagine this isn't his best day, either.

"Maybe I was a little impulsive, but he's here now. Give him time. If you don't like him, I was given a thirty-day money-back guarantee."

Did she really say that? Like he's a new piece of exercise equipment? I've never seen this side of my mother. Connections with the black market? What has she gotten herself into?

When I lift my wrist to continue my discussion with my mom, I see she's turned off her receiver. Shit.

When it comes to business, my mom is a titan of industry. She's thorough and honest and doesn't back down. And she's scrupulous about rules. Why . . . Then it hits me. She's been crying lately and watching one old romance movie after another.

Damn her. She's so fucking misguided, but she did this for me. Every time we talk lately, she tells me how much she wants me to find love. But does she really expect me to find love with this disgusting blue reptile? And did she think this sentient being was going to forget he's been jailed in our guest house living room?

During our whole shouting match, I've looked around for avenues of escape, searched for implements of destruction, and studiously avoided looking at the male in the cage. Now I inspect him.

He's wearing a thick velvet-like crimson uniform with gold piping. It looks military. I'm carefully avoiding his eyes, though, afraid to see the blazing anger in his glare.

Finally lifting my gaze from his clothes to his face, I'm struck by how extremely alien he is. I put in my application for both of the other two available species and was prepared to wait years for one to become available. I couldn't imagine myself with a Draal —they give me the skeeves.

His skin is reptilian, his patterning an interesting variegation of sky blue and royal blue. His lips are thin, his nose is flatter than a human's, and I don't see any ears at all. They must be internal.

The only thing vaguely human about his face are his piercing blue eyes. They seem to have humanity. I decide to focus on them, but can't sustain it for more than a second. Assuming Draals have the same body language as humans, if looks could kill I'd be dead.

He's standing in a military 'at ease' pose, his arms crossed behind his back, his legs wide. I think he's been standing like that a while.

"Um, hi?" I say. This is awkward.

He gives me the slightest nod, seems to try to stare a hole right through me, presses his lips more tightly together, and flares his little slit-like nostrils.

I haven't been in the guest house in years. I used to play here all the time as a kid. It had old furniture and I used it as a playhouse. In addition to the renovations, the furniture is new.

The front door opens into the main room, which is a cozy den. It's flanked by the kitchen on one side and the bedroom with an ensuite bathroom on the other.

The alien's cage, maybe five by five, is near the half-wall that separates the kitchen from the den.

"I'm Annora," I say as I look past him to the gardens outside the French doors. I'm still avoiding the accusation in his gaze.

"Zorn," his voice has the slightest hiss. Not as bad as I would have expected.

Returning to the kitchen, I aimlessly open cabinets, not really looking for anything, just not knowing what to do with myself while a caged Draalian male watches my every move. The reptile's gaze is on me as I rummage. It would be rude to go hide in the bedroom, although I'd really like to throw myself on the bed and have a good cry.

Mom stocked the kitchen with all my favorite comfort foods, so I pull out a box of brownie mix and start cooking. I know I could use the 3-D food printer, but every step of the baking process soothes me.

Once my fingers are busy, my jumbled thoughts begin to take shape. At the top of my awareness is anger. It's hot and spikes through me, then quickly morphs into sadness that pricks tears behind my eyes. I have to swallow a few times, my back to my guest, to get that under control. I don't do 'powerless' well.

I stop in the middle of brownie-making to check all the doors again, being careful to skirt Zorn's cage—God, I'd hate me if I were him—then slide the brownies into the oven.

"I need to piss," he says, his tone firm and direct.

He's in a cage with nothing, not even a chair, and certainly no toilet.

"How long have you been here?"

"I don't understand this planet's passage of time, but I slept here last night. On the floor. We entered your atmosphere yesterday. I was allowed to clean up, then not-so-gently forced into a cage a fourth this size and transported here in the back of a surface vehicle."

Although his voice is matter-of-fact, it suddenly dawns on me that this is a sentient being, far from his home, and he's just standing there. He needs to pee and is probably hungry.

"I'm afraid to open your cage," I admit.

"Do you want me to piss on your floor?" he asks, tilting his head slightly. I don't think this is sarcasm, just a sincere question.

"No! Um, wait."

I grab a pot, bring it to him, then realize it won't fit through the bars. Scurrying back to the kitchen, I grab a tall glass and set it through the bars while safely remaining as far from him as I can. Wanting to give him privacy, I head toward the bedroom, but before I get there, I hear his soft, "I'll need another."

On my way to the kitchen to get him another glass, he says, "Do you have a facility for this? Wouldn't that be more . . . hygienic?"

I'm no more than five feet from his cage when I look at him. His body's stiff, his face is stoic, but his eyes spear me with this request. His tight jaw tells me how much this exchange is costing him. It's almost as if I can feel the hot blaze of his humiliation.

Closing my eyes, I have a long debate with myself. I can't keep this guy in a cage for thirty days. I'm going to have to let him out sometime.

"I'd like to let you out, but I'm afraid."

He nods. "You probably should be. Most sentient beings don't take kindly to being stolen from their planet, shipped across the galaxy, and imprisoned without a sleeping platform or even a pot to piss in."

"Really? You don't want to be on Earth? You were stolen from your home? I thought only volunteers were brought here."

"Your mother used the phrases 'black market' and 'cages'. What about that didn't you understand?"

"Shit! I'm so sorry. Zorn, I'd like to let you out of your cage. Promise you won't kill me." I need to get over my own feelings of shock, anger and betrayal and somehow try to make this right with this poor guy. I thought *I* didn't do powerless well? What about him? He's obviously military and doesn't look used to asking for anything, much less having to beg for a glass to pee in.

"I will tolerate this situation without harming you for the thirty days your mother promised. My planet venerates women and aggressing upon one is prohibited. After thirty days, however, I will follow my military training and try to escape by any means necessary."

"Okay. That's more than I deserve."

"Actually, it's more than your mother deserves. I have no quarrel with you."

There was a note on the kitchen counter saying the cage was locked to my biometrics, so I press my fingertip to the lock, and the door springs open.

For a swift moment I consider running and hiding behind the half-wall to the kitchen, but decide I have to trust him or I'll have to keep him locked up for the entire month.

After I point to the bathroom which is through the bedroom door, he picks up the glass full of his urine and goes to do his business.

I hadn't realized I was crying until a tear slides near the corner of my mouth. This is the worst situation I've ever been in. Worse than when I was little and got picked last for every sport, or got made fun of because of my weight.

"Your eyes are leaking," he says as he stands in the bedroom doorway, his broad shoulder leaning against the frame, empty glass in hand.

Dashing my tears with my knuckle, I admit, "I'm crying."

"They taught me about that while in stasis on the trip here. It's a human expression of sadness."

"Yes."

"What are you sad about?"

Incredulous, my eyes widen as both hands raise to indicate everything around me. "This."

"The situation? I don't find it sad. My feeling is closer to rage."

I step back, several paces. "Are you threatening me?"

"Unless you're a good actress, I think you're a victim here, too. I already said I won't harm you in any way. I'm a male of my word."

Nodding, I say, "So you're willing to make the best of this situation for the next thirty days?"

"Yes."

Look at him, he's practically vibrating with anger, but he's keeping a tight lid on it and promises he won't harm me. If he can handle this situation with aplomb, so can I.

"Hungry?" I ask.

Zorn

Right before my abduction, I saw advertisements on my planet inviting us to come to Earth. I considered it for a moment, then my duty to my planet overrode my desire for a mate. That and the fact I found Earth females unappealing.

I assess my 'host'. To me, hair seems like an evolutionary throwback, kind of primitive. Her skin is . . . bland. And what are the ears for? They seem superfluous, although I learned about sunglasses and I guess they have to rest somewhere to stay on the face. Draalians have nictitating eyelids, a filmy membrane that sweeps from side to side in addition to the eyelid. I'm certain they work better than something you have to carry with you.

I'll keep my promise not to hurt her. Staying thirty days? That won't happen. As soon as I feel my clutchmate Zoriss through my psychic connection, I'll break out of here and find him. I worry he might be in trouble—I haven't felt him since the moment after he escaped.

"Want a brownie?" she asks.

Is that what I smell? It's sickening, like overripe fruit.

I'm hungry. I've been out of stasis over a day and haven't been fed. I could normally go longer, but all I've had during the three prior months on the vessel was chemical nutrition. I don't know what type of animals they eat on Earth, but it doesn't smell promising. I open my mouth for my forked tongue to scent the air, but the better I smell it, the less appetizing it seems.

"Brownie? Is this a . . . pet?"

So many things about this planet are shocking. The fact they abduct males for their cocks and sperm as we were informed on the space vessel. The fact they expect me to befriend and want to mate the person who kept me in a cell. And now, eating a family pet? Even the most primitive societies don't eat the animals they give names to.

"Pet? No. This is a dessert. Normally we eat it after a meal, but I . . ." She shakes her head, then looks up at me, cheeks pinkening. "I stress-eat."

I don't understand stress-eating, but I do understand shame, which she seems to be experiencing. After I take one bite of brownie, I put my utensil down and wonder what's the proper thing to do with food you have to spit out of your mouth. I stalk to the sink and spit, then put my mouth under the nozzle and rinse for a long time.

"You consider that food?" I ask when I return to the table, noting Annora has finished her brownie and is scraping her plate with the tines of her utensil.

"Yes. You don't eat sweets?"

"No." Could that possibly provide nutrients? "Do you have protein in this dwelling? Preferably live although I'll eat it cooked. No household pets, though." That's a line I cannot cross.

She cocks her head and I watch as many emotions sail across her face. The blandness of her features allows me to read her more easily than those of my species. She looks surprised, then offended, then, after a moment of thought, she's amused. Her gaze touches mine for the swiftest moment as she laughs.

She jumps up and programs the food synthesizer. A minute later she pulls out a large plate with what looks like a cooked piece of animal muscle. She sets it in front of me with a dull, round-ended knife. I guess her mother didn't want anything sharp in the house.

"This calls for another brownie while they're still warm," she announces as I attack the first non-liquid nourishment I've had in months. After she rises to slide another brownie from the pan, she cocks her head and asks, "From your hasty trip to the sink, I assume you don't want seconds?"

"I'll pass. The meat is delicious, thank you." I don't mention that anything would taste heavenly after going this long without solid food, well, except for the brownie.

I was too busy spitting out my brownie to see her eat her first one. Now I watch as she takes her first bite. She looks at the brown food—I understand the name now—as if it's a lover, then fills her fork with a perfect square and moves it to her mouth. The tip of her little pink tongue flicks out to touch it, then the whole bite slides into her mouth.

Her eyes drift closed as she chews, like it's the most delicious thing she's ever tasted. Her head cants back an inch as she makes the quietest moan of enjoyment.

What is she doing? I don't understand this female. One minute she is terrified I'll attack her and now she's . . . moaning in the presence of a male? I've never been with a female, but this is not the behavior I would expect from someone who finds me repulsive. Perhaps this is normal behavior on Earth.

She dishes up her next bite, opens her mouth, and nibbles a piece off the end of the brown square. My half-eaten meat is forgotten. I can't tear my eyes from the action. Now that I'm over my initial shock, I decide this is better than the best vid I've ever watched. Compelling. I can't wait to see her next move.

My cocks are hard. I don't quite understand why, moments after being freed from a cage subsequent to being abducted and hauled across the galaxy like livestock, my body is preparing to mount my captor, but that seems to be my response.

At her next nibble, when that delightful tongue which is so different from mine licks her fork, I actually squirm in my chair and can't contain the quiet hiss that escapes my throat.

Her eyes dart to me, then race away. She seems startled, like she forgot I was here. A moment later, they drift back to me. Her awareness is heightened. She might not have been conscious of how her actions affected me before, but I'm pretty sure she knows I'm aroused now.

"This brownie is delicious." Her words are innocent as she over-enunciates the last three syllables, but her voice is deep, low, rough.

"It *looks* delicious." I'm not looking at the brownie, though. I'm looking at those plump, pink alien lips.

Now that she knows she's caught my attention, she's eating differently than before. Her bites are smaller, and her enjoyment is more dramatic—accompanied by frequent moans.

I grunt, unable to contain it. My cocks are straining against the fly of my pants. If I was alone, I'd be rubbing myself to completion right this moment, but I sit glued to the spot, watching the sexiest vid of my life. Only this is real. And it's taking place three feet away from me.

She takes the last bite, swirling it around in her mouth as if it were a sip of expensive wine. After she swallows, the tip of her tongue peeks out and licks first her top lip, then the bottom. Then she spears me with a look so sensual, so full of heat it's as if her hand is gripping my primary cock.

Then I feel it, the telltale twinge of my internal testicles signaling my imminent release. I rise from my seat and run to the bathroom. Barely getting there in time to spurt into the toilet with a hiss loud enough to be heard back on Draal.

Leaning one hand against the wall over the toilet, every muscle in my body goes limp as I wonder how that just happened. I don't recall ever coming without touching myself before.

I'm a captain in the Draalian army. Discipline and self-control define who I am and who I've been for fifteen years. The human doesn't even appeal to me. She finds me repulsive.

It makes sense, though, that my cocks would be hard for her; I've never been around a female who wasn't a relative. The few females who are still being born on Draal are cloistered and protected.

Any normal male who'd never been within ten feet of a female before would be ready to rut their worst enemy under these circumstances. Add to it the way she slipped her delicate pink tongue over her full lips, the flirty smile, the heated glances? And don't even mention her sounds of pleasure. My behavior makes perfect sense. I'm just a normal Draalian male.

Although she was spawned by the devil incarnate, Annora seems like a nice female. She's never been around a male—ever. The download I received said the few elderly males still living on her planet are in armed barracks for their own protection from the virus. Perhaps she, just like me, is reacting to being within ten feet of someone of the opposite sex for the first time in her life. Even one she doesn't find attractive.

I have to admit that whatever caused it, I wouldn't mind if it happened again. Only next time perhaps she could participate more fully. As I imagine her hand with its soft pink fingers gripping one, or both, of my blue cocks, they respond to my fantasy.

"Don't forget she's the enemy," I whisper to myself in the mirror, then jam my cocks in my pants and stride back into the kitchen.

She's still sitting at the table, looking interested. Her brow is cocked in question. I don't respond. We both know what just happened. I have no need to talk about it, nor to cover it up.

"It looks like maybe you like brownies after all," she tosses her head and smiles.

"I think I'm developing a taste for them. Yes."

"Zorn," she says as she holds my gaze for the first time since she was pushed through the front door. "Carpe diem!"

Her face is alive with happiness, although I have no idea what she just said.

"That means seize the day in an antique, dusty language. Let's do it, Zorn. This whole situation sucks. Neither of us can leave, but we *can* choose to make it better. I don't want to worry you're going to kill me in my sleep. And I don't want you to worry that I'll feed you my dog or take away your bathroom privileges or lock you in a cage.

"Let's figure out a way to do this without killing each other. No. Better than that, let's figure out a way to have fun for thirty days. When was the last time you had a vacation?"

"I'd just returned to Draal the day I was stolen. Prior to that, it was five years."

"It's been a while for me, too. How about this? You teach me Draalian games, I'll teach you some from Earth. You teach me how to cook some foods you like to eat, and I'll show you some of mine. I promise not even one dish will contain a family pet." She smiles and winks at me. "We'll have a staycation."

Although I don't know what a staycation is, I do know that her features aren't pinched anymore, and she seems excited about it. If she's happy, perhaps she'll be distracted enough for me to escape.

"Staycation it is!"

BUY LOVE UNCAGED HERE!

WELCOME TO EARTH
WHERE THE LOVE IS ON US!

Love Uncaged
AWOL Alien
Sweet Dreams
Trophy of the Dragon
Dubious Treasure
Her Unsuitable Suitor
Love on Impact

ABOUT THE AUTHOR

Alana Khan writes under a pen name because until recently she was a practicing psychotherapist and didn't want to scandalize her clients with the steamy stories she writes for fun. Her history as a therapist gives her unique insight into people's thoughts, feelings and motivations. It provides her writing the ring of truth and deep emotion.

Many of her characters have been scarred and traumatized. They have to work hard to earn their happily ever after, which is guaranteed in every book—they deserve it.

https://www.alanakhan.com/

MORE FROM ALANA KHAN

Galaxy Gladiators Alien Abduction Romance Series

Galaxy Sanctuary Alien Abduction Romance Series

Cosmic Kissed (Earthbound Alien Romance Series)

Galaxy Pirates Alien Abduction Romance Series

Mastered by the Zinn Alien Abduction Romance Series

Treasured by the Zinn Alien Abduction Romance Series

Billionaire Doms of Blackstone

BOX SETS

Galaxy Gladiators Alien Abduction Romance Series Books 1 to 3

Galaxy Gladiators Alien Abduction Romance Series Books 1 to 4

First In Series - Zar / Sextus / Arzz

Treasured by the Zinn Alien Abduction Romance Series

Mastered by the Zinn Alien Abduction Romance Series

Printed in Great Britain
by Amazon